A FAREWELL TO YARNS

"Agatha Christie is alive and well and writing mysteries under the name Jill Churchill."
Nancy Pickard,
award-winning author of the JENNY CAIN mysteries

"Tart and clever . . . As much fun as settling in for a cozy gossip with your best friend . . . A delightful mystery romp."
Carolyn G. Hart, author of *The Christie Caper*

And coming soon from Avon Books:
GRIME & PUNISHMENT

"A winner!"
Elizabeth Peters

"Jane Jeffry is a cross between Miss Marple and Erma Bombeck."
Mysteries By Mail

"Written with a generous helping of wit, Churchill leaves us eagerly awaiting the promised sequel."
Alfred Hitchcock's Mystery Magazine

"Great fun . . . Churchill does for GRIME what Isaacs did for COMPROMISING POSITIONS."
Tulsa Sunday World

A FAREWELL TO YARNS

A Jane Jeffry Mystery

JILL CHURCHILL

AVON BOOKS ◆ NEW YORK

A FAREWELL TO YARNS is an original publication of Avon Books. This work has never before appeared in book form. This work is a novel. Any similarity to actual persons or events is purely coincidental.

AVON BOOKS
A division of
The Hearst Corporation
1350 Avenue of the Americas
New York, New York 10019

First Avon Books Printing: December 1991

AVON TRADEMARK REG. U.S. PAT. OFF. AND IN OTHER COUNTRIES, MARCA REGISTRADA, HECHO EN CANADA.

Printed in Canada

UNV 10

Dedicated to
Barbara Mertz,
the acerbic fairy godmother
who brought Jane back to life
And with thanks to
Gladys Staab
and the Shawnee Mission
Garden club

----------1----------

December 10, 8:37 A.M.

The Jeffry house in the suburbs of Chicago was empty, but it was a hectic sort of emptiness. The portable television in the kitchen was on the "Today" show at top volume. Jane's ninth-grade daughter, Katie, had turned it on in the desperate hope of finding some tidbit of news with which to complete her social studies assignment. Naturally, she hadn't thought of turning it off before leaving for school. Such things never occurred to Katie. From upstairs, the sound of sixteen-year-old Mike's stereo was blaring an extremely noisy Queen album. Mike didn't set much store by turning things off, either.

The coffee maker was making a very peculiar burble because, in her haste to get her kids off to school, Jane had slopped water on the heating element. The furnace was going full blast, making the funny clicking sound Jane had been worrying about for a couple of days, and from the basement there was the sound of some lonely item of clothing with a metal button thrashing around in the dryer.

The kitchen phone was ringing insistently and was being ignored by the cat closest to it. He, a rotund gray tabby tom named Max, was standing in the sink fishing expertly in the garbage disposal for any little treasures

1

that might not have been thoroughly disposed of. The faucet was dripping every few seconds on the back of his almost nonexistent neck, but it didn't seem to worry him. His counterpart, a sleek yellow item named Meow, was daintily cruising the breakfast room table for crumbs.

In the dining room a great shambling dog named Willard was barking his head off at the neighbor who walked the poodle by the house every morning. Willard had been soundly trounced once by the poodle and now spent a few refreshing moments every morning telling the interloper (from the safety of his own dining room) what would happen to him next time they met. Jane had to clean the low windows at least once a week because of his spitty morning barkfests.

Added to this at 8:38 was the rumble of Jane's car pulling into the driveway. "It's only a little hole in the muffler, Mom," Mike had assured her. Jane thought it sounded like the Concorde taking off every time she accelerated.

Jane Jeffry came in the outside kitchen door a moment later. Normally an attractive (though she didn't really think so) and well-groomed woman in her late thirties, this morning Jane was a wreck. Most of her blond hair was stuffed under a stocking cap that did more to emphasize than conceal its uncombed condition. She wore an antique and very tatty so-called mink she'd picked up at a garage sale several years earlier. Jane didn't really approve of wearing fur—her economics as well as ethics were offended by it—but this one looked like it came from an animal that *ought* to be extinct. The coat was a disgrace, and she knew it, but it was incredibly warm, just what she needed for driving winter morning car pools. With this unstylish garment, she wore jeans, a sweatshirt that said, "This is no ordinary housewife you're dealing with," and sheepskin slippers that she removed and shook the snow from into the sink—after hoisting Max out.

She leaned on the counter for a moment, looking around the kitchen with disgust. "This looks like white trash lives here, and it's your fault!" she told the cat. Then she bellowed at the dog, "Willard! I'll bring that poodle in here to beat you up if you don't stop barking this instant!"

There was a knock at the kitchen door, and Jane opened it to find her friend and next-door neighbor Shelley Nowack. A few snowflakes spangled Shelley's neat cap of dark hair and the velvet trim on her coat. In honor of the approaching holidays, she had a sequined Christmas tree brooch pinned to her lapel. Even in her distracted state, Jane noticed that Shelley's high-heeled boots were of exactly the same shade as her gloves and her purse. "How dare you look that good already."

"My God, Jane. What happened to you? You look like you've been savaged by a gang of bikers."

". . . which is roughly equivalent to being the mother of three kids. The electricity must have been out for an hour or so last night. We overslept. Why didn't you?"

"My alarm is battery powered. You should have one. Now I know what to get you for Christmas."

"I should have a lot of things. A housekeeper for starters. Then maybe an indulgent millionaire husband. Shelley, pour us some coffee, would you?"

Shelley took off her coat, folding it neatly over the back of a chair, then laid her gloves and purse on the seat. She took down two coffee mugs from the shelf, while Jane hastily cleaned the table. "Calm down. We've got plenty of time," Shelley said as Jane brutally shoved cereal boxes into the cabinet.

"Yes, I guess so. I just woke up in a panic mode and can't seem to stop." She sat down and blew on the coffee. "Jesus! I hate days that start this way. Mike thought they ought to just stay home from school altogether since they were going to be late anyway and was outraged that I wouldn't consider it. Katie acted like I'd turned the clocks off on purpose to make her miss some girly-girly gossip session in the second floor john before school. And Todd took advantage of the situation to trick me into signing a sheet saying I'd help drive the fifth grade to something or other. If Steve weren't already dead, I'd kill him for leaving me with all this. He should have been here helping."

"Come on, Jane. Steve wouldn't have been helping you this morning. He'd have been standing around helplessly, wanting you to iron a shirt or something."

"You're right. Either way, I'm mad at him. Ughhh! This coffee is awful."

"That's possibly Steve's fault, too," Shelley said with a grin.

Jane smiled back. "As a matter of fact, it is. I buy it because it was *his* favorite brand. He's been gone nearly a year, and I'm still drinking his disgusting coffee. What's the matter with me?"

"Nothing that time won't take care of. Just think. You can use some of his lovely insurance money to buy all sorts of expensive gourmet brands to try out. Now, go get dressed and put on a face, and I'll tidy up the kitchen."

"Don't even think about it! I don't want you to look in my cabinets and know what a slob I really am."

Shelley put a well-manicured hand on Jane's wrist and said, "Can I be honest?"

"Why stop at honest? Go straight to cruel."

"I don't have to look into cabinets to know your secret. Get dressed, unless you plan to meet your old friend looking this way."

"I don't think Phyllis would care. Knowing Phyllis,

it's questionable whether she'd notice, but I'd hate to risk seeing a look of raw pity in her eyes. I'll have to feed Willard; he'd be terrified to eat anything someone else's hands had touched. The whole world is out to poison him, he says, but the cat food is under the sink in the guest bathroom.''

"There must be a reason for that,'' Shelley said mildly, having long since accepted most of the vagaries of Jane's peculiar housekeeping system.

"It's my emergency supply, for when I've run out and they start attacking my ankles.'' Jane disappeared down the basement steps, peeling her sweatshirt off over her head as she went.

She came back up a few minutes later wearing a denim skirt and blue-and-white striped blouse. "There's nothing like getting dressed right out of the dryer. So toasty and warm.'' She sat down on a kitchen chair and struggled into a pair of panty hose. The cats were sitting on opposite sides of their dish, staring at each other, each afraid to eat first for fear of getting smacked on the head by the other. Willard kept sticking his big wet nose into the back of Jane's knees. "Yes, yes. Just a minute,'' she told him.

As she stood up to give her panty hose a final tug, her finger punched through the hose, and a fat run slithered down her leg. "A man invented panty hose,'' Shelley observed.

"Probably a grandson of the man who invented corsets!'' Jane said, stripping off the ruined item and throwing it into the wastebasket. She hurriedly fed Willard, then ran upstairs while Shelley continued to tidy the kitchen.

When Jane returned, she was a new person. Her short, streaked blond hair was combed and sprayed into a tousled upswept style—Shelley had made her go to a hairdresser to learn how to create this miracle—and she had on navy knee-length boots that added a full two inches to her height. With makeup, she looked a good five years younger and a great deal less stressed. "You do clean up good," Shelley said approvingly.

Jane glanced around the spotless kitchen. "So do you. If Paul ever goes bankrupt and you need a job, I'll hire you."

"The sad thing is, I'd love it," Shelley observed. "I know it's shallow of me, but I really love to clean. It's not anything compulsive, it's just that you can see a difference when you're through. Not like raising kids or something that you're not sure how it's going to turn out for a couple of decades."

Jane sat down and took another sip of the now-cold coffee. "And I hate cleaning, because no matter how often or well you do it, it has to be done again—and again and again. How are we on time?"

"Plenty. Your friend's flight isn't due for an hour and a half, and it's only an hour to the airport."

"Still, I'd like to get going. Do you mind?"

"Not a bit. Are you driving, or shall I?"

This question raised a good number of conflicting emotions in Jane. Though Shelley was normally the most calm, refined individual in the world, something about getting behind the steering wheel of a car brought out a savage, competitive streak in her. On the other hand, Jane didn't think her muffler would stick with her all the way to O'Hare, and she had an awful suspicion that the kids had left McDonald's wrappers and other trash in the backseat, where Phyllis would have to ride. Of course, Phyllis Wagner was so down-to-earth that she probably wouldn't think a thing about it. The deciding factor was really the afghan—

"Why don't you drive so I can crochet?" Jane said after a moment of consideration. "I've lied to Fiona. I told her I've finished it already and have just forgotten to bring it over. I've got to get the damned thing done."

"Can you crochet and ride?"

"With you? I'd rather crochet than watch." Jane went into the living room and grabbed a big yellow plastic bag that contained the afghan-in-progress.

Shelley followed her. "Why don't you have a tree up yet?"

"I'll get one in a day or two. You could at least notice and appreciate all those boxes in the corner. Those are the Christmas decorations, fresh from the basement and ready to go up whenever I have a spare day or two."

True to form, Shelley made a spectacularly belligerent entry onto the main road at the bottom of their street. Jane didn't even look up from the snarl of red, green, and white yarn in her lap. She just leaned with the motion of the minivan and went on muttering, "Triple, triple, triple, single. Triple, triple, triple, single, single. Triple—"

"Hold it, Jane. You just did two singles," Shelley said.

"I was turning a corner."

"I suppose that makes sense. What I don't understand is why you have to talk your way through crocheting."

"For the simple reason that I'm not very good at it. Saying the stitches out loud is the only way I can keep track of where I am and what I'm doing."

Shelley made what she called a "running stop" at a stop sign and said, "You must be a lot of fun around the fireside in the evenings."

Jane stopped working for a moment. "Firesides would be okay. It's the television that gets me in trouble. The kids won't let me in the same room when they're watching. I annoy them to a frenzy."

"Of course you do. Just being their mother is enough for that."

"I can't understand what went wrong with me. The women in my family were usually born knitting. You know those little hats babies wear home from the hospital . . . ? My aunts made their own to wile away time in the bassinets. I swear it. Knitting and crocheting are in our genes. Even Katie can whip up a granny square. How could I pass the ability on to my daughter without any sticking to me? My mother can work an elaborate cable stitch in three colors without even looking at the needles and discuss the history of the Reformation at the same time. I must be missing some crucial part of my brain."

"The part that connects with your hands probably. Or maybe the part that wants to discuss the Reformation. We're only a block from Fiona's. I've got all that stuff I have to drop off for the church bazaar. We have time before we have to be at the airport?"

"And have you speed all the way to make up lost time? I'd rather go to a dentist than let myself in for that. No, I'll help you unload it at Fiona's later. Fiona's another one—she could build a whole town with left-over scraps of yarn if she set her mind to it. Of course, she's English, so that helps explain it. Probably cut her teeth on the Bayeux Tapestry."

"Isn't that in France?"

Jane cocked an eyebrow. "If you're going to get literal on me, I won't be your friend anymore."

"If you're not my friend, I won't drive you to the airport to pick up this long lost pal of yours and you'll never finish that afghan—which might be my ultimate contribution to the long-term benefit of mankind. Now, tell me about this friend of yours."

—— 2 ——

"Phyllis Wagner was from somewhere back East and had come to Chicago to live with an aunt when she was a teenager. When we were both newlyweds, we were neighbors," Jane said, hanging onto the afghan and trying to work without consciously thinking about it. Surely it was possible. Surely a grown woman who could manage the rococo complexities of carpooling three kids could crochet without talking to herself.

"We lived in a ratty apartment building in the city. Mostly elderly people and students. You know the kind of place. Steve was still in school then, and I was working at one of his family's pharmacies."

"Was Phyllis a student, too?"

"No, Phyllis wasn't the student type. And she didn't work either. Back in those days, if you recall, women weren't expected to, unless it was absolutely necessary. As far as I could tell, she spent her days visiting with other people in the building. She brightened a lot of lives. In the evenings she visited me or we went to movies or something. Steve was studying all the time and hardly noticed that I was gone."

"And Phyllis's husband?"

"She'd only married Chet Wagner a few months before they moved into the apartment building. He was much older. Phyllis was only nineteen or so, and Chet must have been in his mid-thirties. That seemed down-

9

right ancient to me then. Chet was never home either. As I recall, he'd lost everything, including his sons and his business, in a divorce and was starting over. That's why they were slumming it with us. He was involved in starting a company that had something to do with computers.''

"Not a bad time to start in computers.''

"I'll say. He made an absolute fortune in no time. We all lived there for six months or so, then Steve graduated, and I discovered I was pregnant with Mike, and we started building the house. About the same time we moved out here, Phyllis and Chet moved into a little house in Evanston. The next thing I knew, she'd moved into a bigger house. I was there for lunch one day, and it was a gorgeous place. Phyllis and I kept in touch, but sort of loosely. She didn't have any children, except Chet's boys on vacations, and I think that was sort of difficult. I had Mike just after we moved here, and then Katie came along, and I was knee-deep in babies and diapers and sterilizers. I couldn't fit into my prepregnancy clothes and couldn't afford nice new ones to fit into her lifestyle. And you remember what it was like, being so absorbed in your babies that you lost touch with the rest of the world.''

Shelley bullied her way skillfully through a knot of cars and said, "Boy, do I remember those days. It always took three people to cram me into the outfit I took to the hospital to wear home.''

"Actually, it wasn't that Phyllis would have cared if I'd turned up in baggy jeans and a sweatshirt. I'll say that for her. No matter how much money Chet made, she stayed Phyllis. Fortunately—or unfortunately. She always seemed to think the money was sort of nice but didn't quite know why they needed so much of it. Frankly, it made me jealous sometimes. There we were, struggling for nickels, and Phyllis sort of shed cash like water off a duck. It wasn't her fault, and I didn't blame her, but it did create a barrier between us.

"Anyway, we saw less and less of each other and then talked on the phone less often, and finally, when Katie was a baby, Phyllis had some sort of breakdown. I never knew quite why—we weren't ever really close enough to talk about gut-level stuff. I never thought Phyllis *had* a gut level, to be honest. She was such a simple, straightforward person. Chet took her on some sort of cruise to recover, and the next time I heard from her, it was in a letter telling me they'd stayed on a little island in the Caribbean that they loved so much that Chet bought it."

"Bought the whole island?"

"Well, most of it, I think. There was a resort hotel and a little village where the hotel workers lived, but they owned the rest, as I understand. I got the impression from her later letters that they eventually bought the hotel as well and put up a few houses for friends and business associates of Chet's."

"An island in the Caribbean and she comes to Illinois in December? Is she crazy?"

"Homesick, I suspect. I don't know why, after all these years, she'd be so anxious to come back, but she is. We write long letters at Christmas and send the occasional birthday card, but that's all. Or it was until last winter. Somehow she heard about Steve dying—"

"From that distance? Not to speak ill of the dead, but Steve's passing was hardly an international event."

Jane smiled. Most of her acquaintances went miles out of their way to avoid mentioning Steve and would never refer to his death. Only a true friend like Shelley would speak casually, even lightly, about it. Life, not to mention conversation, was so much easier with a real friend.

"I don't know how she knew. I suspect she's always

taken the Chicago papers, though, because in her letters she frequently mentions local events as if she's familiar with them. She may do it for the sake of Chet's sons. One of them lives somewhere close to us, or used to. She mentioned him a couple times, and I suppose she hoped I'd make an effort to meet him, but I never did. You don't know any Wagners in the neighborhood, do you?''

"Hmmm, there's a Joannie Wagner with a fourth grader. I worked at the school carnival with her.''

"That sounds familiar. Anyway, Phyllis called immediately after Steve died and offered to come stay with me, since my mother was having that surgery and couldn't be here.''

"Oh, I think I do remember you mentioning her. I think I answered the phone that day.''

"Could be. Of course, I had you and Steve's mother, Thelma, and didn't need her—didn't even want her, to be truthful. Phyllis was really a virtual stranger to me by that time. But a month or so later, when I was getting back to being able to think and talk a little, she called again and asked if I'd like to bring the children down to their island for a visit. I begged off, and I must have inadvertently given the impression that I couldn't afford to go. Not that I could have afforded it, but that wasn't the reason. So in the next mail there was a registered letter containing four plane tickets.''

"You never mentioned that to me! Why didn't you go?''

"I didn't tell you, because I was afraid you'd make me go. I couldn't pull myself together and figure out what to do about the dog and the cats and clothes and stopping the paper. You know what a zombie I was for a while. Besides, I—well, I just didn't want to spread my grief around. The only place I felt I could heal was at home.''

Shelley nodded her understanding.

"I sent the tickets back with the gooiest thank-you I could write," Jane went on. "She returned a heart-breakingly sweet letter, very understanding, saying how she'd been selfish to try to get me there, but she'd missed me so much all those years. Of course, I had to write and offer to have her visit here after all she'd done, or tried to do for me. To my astonishment, she took me up on it. Not then, but she said she'd like to visit this winter. So, here we are, picking her up. I don't know why she's not visiting Chet's son and his Joannie instead of me. I don't think they're close, but she's never indicated that they don't get along. Although, as boys, when she and Chet were first married, his sons gave her trouble. One of them—John, I think his name was—was especially close to his father."

"So what's Phyllis like? Will she be fun or intolerable?"

Jane had the crochet hook in her teeth as she rewound the yarn. She took it out and tapped her knee reflectively. "Just boring, I would guess. She's very nice. Very, very nice. She's the kind of person you absolutely cannot dislike. But it's equally impossible to be crazy about her, and that's always made me feel a little guilty. I feel I *ought* to like her much better than I do. She's a truly good person who deserves the kind of friendship you and I have. I feel obligated, but unwilling, to provide it. She's rather quiet. I remember her as a sort of country girl come to the city, even though she grew up in Boston or Washington or someplace. She had that sort of wide-eyed, half-scared, half-thrilled look most of the time."

"Certainly she's outgrown that by now. I don't think I could stand dewy innocence," Shelley said. "Why is she coming without her husband? Doing a little Christmas shopping or something?"

"Probably so. She's coming by way of New York; I guess she was there for a few days. She's probably dropped a couple million already. But I do find this trip odd. She and Chet have always been inseparable. In her last letter there was the merest hint of trouble in paradise. I'd hate to see her marriage go bad. She doesn't deserve that kind of unhappiness and—I guess it's selfish of me, but I don't think I could stand hours of talk about a disintegrating marriage."

"And you think it is? Disintegrating?"

"I hope not."

"How long is she staying?"

"She didn't say. I imagine two or three days. Well, we can get her busy on the bazaar. She'll like that, unless she's changed a lot. She was always making some little ornamental something. She's another of those damned born knitters, and she's the only person I've ever met of our generation who knows how to do tatting."

"Tatting! I thought it was a lost art."

"The year we lived in the apartment she made Christmas tree ornaments for everybody in the building with styrofoam balls and sequins with all this starched, tatted lace. Sounds tacky, but they were beautiful. All those lonely old people in the building were very touched. So was I. I still have mine."

"Then she'll fit right in with the church bazaar crowd. They'll think you imported her especially for their use."

Jane was quiet for a moment. They were approaching the airport, and the sky was full of planes. "Say—the bazaar reminds me of something else. Phyllis was madly in love with Richie Divine. She'll be interested in meeting Fiona—the famous widow. Phyllis had a scrapbook of her favorite stars and another one just for Richie. I thought that was strange, but sort of endearing, that a grown—well, married woman would keep fan scrapbooks.''

Shelley didn't say anything, just rolled her eyes. Jane looked sideways at her, and added, "She also did jigsaw puzzles, pictures of puppies and kittens, and poured glue over them so she could hang them up on the walls.''

"Good God, Jane! You can't mean that!''

Jane giggled. "No, I just wanted to see if you were paying attention.''

"What terminal are we going to?'' Shelley asked repressively.

"Damn it, Shelley! I've crocheted the door handle into my afghan!''

Jane didn't recognize the slim, expensively dressed woman who waved at her as she moved forward with the crowd at the arrivals gate. "Is that her?'' Shelley asked.

"I guess it must be,'' Jane said through the side of her mouth. She glanced around to see if perhaps the woman was gesturing to someone standing behind her. But no one was reacting. Jane assumed a smile that was welcoming but not committed enough to embarrass her if this wasn't Phyllis.

The crowd got backed up behind a little girl who had tripped and was screaming bloody murder. Jane had time to study the woman she assumed was little Phyllis all grown up and rich. The Phyllis she remembered had mousy brown hair and an air of perpetual disarray just short of sloppiness. This woman was exquisite; expensively frosted hair swirled around a face that could have graced a magazine cover. This was the sort of beautiful, mature woman who was shown in the high fashion fur ads in magazines Jane flipped through at the bookstore but couldn't afford to buy. Tanned. Gorgeous teeth. Gorgeous teeth? Phyllis had disgraceful teeth back in the old Chicago apartment days. It was the one real drawback to her appearance.

As Jane watched, the woman turned to a young man standing slightly behind her. She said something and pointed to Jane. The young man, blond, tanned, smashingly handsome, and unquestionably the most sulky individual in the whole airport, glared.

"Who is that with her?" Shelley asked.

"Dear God! I hope it's somebody she met on the plane," Jane said. She could feel her plaster smile crumbling.

"He couldn't be one of her husband's sons, could he?" Shelley asked.

"Too young. They'd be in their late twenties. That one's not more than eighteen or nineteen. He's probably some flunky of Chet's who was sent along to see her on and off planes."

The woman who might be Phyllis had shifted her carry-on case and several lumpy plastic bags to her left arm and slipped her right arm around the boy in a clearly intimate gesture. He looked like he was straining to get away.

Shelley asked, "You don't suppose he's her lover, do you?"

"Bite your tongue! I've got underwear older than that boy!"

"Well, he's not somebody she picked up on the plane. Look, their hand luggage matches."

"Oh, shit!" Jane said, hissing. "Am I going to have a middle-aged woman cavorting around my house with her gigolo? Oh, Shelley—what will I do? How could she? He's just a kid. How mortifying. How will I explain it to my kids?"

"You won't have to. They'll catch on right away."

"Don't say that! That's what I'm afraid of."

"Then don't call her middle-aged. She's our age."

Jane suddenly felt a wave of sympathetic understanding for the little girl who had tied up traffic and was now sitting, screaming, and kicking her heels on the floor. It was just what Jane wanted to do herself.

3

Somebody picked up the screaming child, cutting off its wails. The crowd surged forward. "Jane! Darling Jane!" Phyllis cried, dragging the young man behind her as she fought through the people blocking her. Jane found herself being embraced, her nose tickled by mink and Phyllis's scent—that of very new hundred-dollar bills dipped in Giorgio. One of Phyllis's plastic bags was caught between them, and Jane was being gouged by something that felt like a knitting needle.

"You haven't changed a bit!" Phyllis said, holding Jane by both arms and studying her.

"You have," Jane blurted out, not sure whether to be flattered or insulted by Phyllis's remark. Jane had hoped that maturity would have improved her.

"No, I haven't," Phyllis said. "It's just my teeth. Chet insisted on having all these porcelain things done to them. He thought it mattered to me, the darling. So I let him think so. It made him happy."

"Phyllis—" It was hard to call her that. Jane wondered how this expensively dressed individual could be the same woman she'd once known. "I'm sorry that Chet didn't come along. How is he?"

At that, Phyllis's eyes began to fill, and her chin trembled almost imperceptibly. "He's just fine, Jane. We just needed some time apart." She sniffed, paused a moment to get a grip on herself.

18

And in that moment, with her chin shaking with incipient tears, the woman before her became the old Phyllis—poor little insecure Phyllis who'd spent her days befriending the old people in the apartment building and making Christmas ornaments. At the same time, Jane realized that her fear of marriage troubles was right, and she was probably in for hours of heart-to-heart girl talk. But for the moment, Phyllis had put aside her own woes to offer sympathy to Jane. "I just can't say how sorry I was about Steve's death. I still can't believe it. You—a widow before forty."

Jane didn't know what to say. She didn't want to talk about widowhood. She certainly wasn't going to tell Phyllis that Steve wouldn't have been out on that icy road in the middle of a bleak February night, except that he was leaving her for another woman. That was something she wouldn't tell Phyllis. Not now or later. "Your teeth are beautiful," she said instead. "That was nice of Chet."

"Oh, but Chet did something much finer for me. I've been dying to tell you, but I made myself wait until I could see your face. Jane, I want you to meet Bobby Bryant."

She dragged the sulky young man forward. Jane had been vaguely aware of him standing in the background, watching their reunion with about as much joy as Jane felt emptying kitty litter. He was even more gorgeous up close. He had thick blond hair, beautifully cut and sun bleached to wheat-colored perfection. His nose might be a little too long and pointed, but it suited his thin, tanned face and didn't distract a bit from a fine, if petulant, mouth. Good God, Katie was going to collapse at the mere sight of him. Jane could see a terrible crush coming. "Hello, Bobby," she said.

He took her hand in a languid grip. It wasn't an effeminate gesture, just a supremely bored one. "Hi," he said listlessly.

"Isn't he handsome?" Phyllis gushed.

"Uh, yes. I'm sure he must be," Jane said, embarrassed at discussing him as if he were a pet.

As she was stumbling around trying to think of what to say next, Shelley nudged her in the ribs and jarred her into further introductions. Phyllis was very polite to Shelley but was obviously eager to get back to discussing Bobby. "Jane, do you know who Bobby is?"

"Come on, Phyl," the young man said. "Do we have to stand here in the middle of everything jawing about this?" Jane was surprised to hear a distinctly Chicago accent in his voice.

"That boy needs a fat lip," Shelley muttered.

Phyllis was hanging onto Bobby, gazing up at him with adoration. Jane was paralyzed with embarrassment. She'd heard about older women taking handsome young lovers. It wasn't something done in her circle, of course. Most of her circle of friends hung out in the school parking lots in their station wagons or in the grocery store. But among the jet set, it was fairly normal to have a tiff with your husband and take up with a pretty boy. Or so she was led to believe by such reliable authorities as *People* magazine and *TV Guide*, Jane's windows on the world.

But it was shocking that sweet, slightly boring Phyllis should have fallen into such pitiful ways. It was odd, too. She seemed genuinely grieved about her problems with Chet, whatever they might be. Even then, it wouldn't be quite so skin-crawling awful if the boy weren't so rude and contemptuous of her. Weren't paid lovers supposed to earn their keep by pretending love? Or at least courtesy? Surely there were rules about that sort of thing.

"Why don't you see about our luggage, darling,

while I talk to Jane and Shelley?'' Phyllis asked him, apparently unoffended by his attitude.

He shrugged and slouched off.

"Isn't he the most darling boy?'' Phyllis marveled, watching him move out of sight. She shifted her plastic bags to her other arm. "Oh, Jane, tell me you think he's wonderful. I couldn't stand it if you don't.''

"Why, Phyllis, how could I say? We just met. But I'm sure you're right,'' Jane said. She could almost feel her nose growing longer as she spoke.

"Can't you tell who he is?'' Phyllis asked. "I don't suppose there's that much resemblance, except in my eyes.''

"Resemblance to whom?'' Shelley asked, seeing that Jane was floundering in confusion.

"To me, of course. He's my son! But surely you'd guessed!''

"Your . . . son? You mean Chet's son?''

"No, Jane. My very own baby boy. Oh, I have managed to surprise you, haven't I? What fun!''

Jane shook her head. "Phyllis, you never had children, and that boy is older than my kids—''

"That's because I had him before you had yours, before I knew you.'' She giggled as if this were a terribly clever remark, then suddenly got very serious. "I just never told anybody. I gave him up for adoption, you see. Before I even knew you. And we've just been reunited for a few wonderful months. It was all Chet's doing—dear, understanding Chet.''

She looked like she was going to go tearful again, and Jane was staring at her as if she'd grown another head. Shelley grabbed Jane's arm and said firmly, "Jane and I will go get the car while you and your son get your luggage. See that hall? Follow that to the doors, and we'll pick you up there, okay?''

Jane was out in the cold air before she started to

gather her wits. "Shelley! What a nightmare! I thought it was terrible enough that he was her lover. It's even more frightening this way. You can dump a pretty boy, but not if he's your son. How utterly ghastly. She actually thinks he's great."

"He's pond scum," Shelley said, striding across the parking area. "Her Chet should have stuck to fixing her teeth. What do you suppose she meant about it being Chet's doing? Is he Chet's kid?"

Jane tried to cast her mind back seventeen years, not an easy thing with all the lively clutter of events that intervened. "I wouldn't think that's possible. Phyllis always made a big deal about how she and Chet had only known each other a month before they were married. All very romantic. I guess she might have been lying, but I don't think she knew how to back then."

"A month would be a pretty quick gestation," Shelley said. She'd found the minivan and was fishing around in the depths of her purse for the keys. She located them, and the two of them piled in. Jane found a battered half pack of cigarettes in her purse. She was trying to cut down on her smoking in the hopes that she'd make it easier to actually quit altogether at some vaguely defined future date. But this called for a cigarette. If she'd been a drinker, it would have called for a fifth of vodka.

Shelley's minivan bolted into traffic, and she said, "Jane, I don't like this. Circles within circles," she added ominously.

"Oh Shelley, the temptation to fling myself out the door in front of traffic is almost too much," she said, puffing so frantically she made herself a little dizzy. "As if the stress of any Christmas, much less my first Christmas as a widow weren't enough . . . You know what this means, don't you? She's bringing that overgrown brat to my house. My *house*! I'll have him drooping around, snarling—Mike will despise him on sight, and I'm afraid Katie will do just the opposite.''

"Well, it won't be forever," Shelley said. "You said she was only staying two or three days.''

"I said that's what I assumed, but obviously my assuming powers aren't at their best. I didn't specify a time limit, and neither did she. Just said she'd be here today. It didn't cross my mind to ask when she'd be leaving. It didn't seem to matter. She's so easy to be around, I figured she'd stay as long as she wanted without being in my way. Oh, what have I done?''

They worked their way through airport traffic. At the entrance to the baggage claim area, Phyllis was standing alone. She got in the backseat of the minivan and was quiet for a minute. She was very pale with bright, angry circles of red on her cheeks.

"Poor Bobby," she finally said, but she didn't sound sympathetic. After a pause, she worked up to tolerant understanding. "I don't think he likes traveling. Of course, he won't admit it, but I wonder if he's afraid of planes. Lots of people are, but a boy his age wouldn't admit it. Yes, I think that must be it. He's been—well, touchy, I guess you'd say, ever since I told him about our plans for Christmas.''

"Your plans for Christmas?" Jane asked, her heart in her mouth.

"Why visiting you, I mean." She started rummaging in her purse for a tissue.

Jane cast Shelley a despairing look and mouthed, "Two weeks!''

"Where is Bobby?" Shelley asked. She was blocking traffic, and people were starting to honk and swerve around her.

"There's some problem with one of his bags," Phyllis said with a definite sniffle.

Jane immediately thought of a drug bust. What might

happen if someone coming to visit her had a suitcase full of cocaine? Would the authorities think she had something to do with it?

"The airline scuffed one of them up horribly, and he's very upset. Bobby isn't used to having nice things, and he's rather fussy about them now. That's only natural."

At this point, Bobby himself came slamming out through the doors with a skycap loaded down with luggage in his wake. Shelley got out, opened the back doors of the minivan, and supervised while Jane and Phyllis sat silently in the car. Jane noticed that Bobby didn't make any move to tip the man, so Shelley took care of it. She'd have to remember to reimburse Shelley later.

Bobby and Shelley reached the driver's door at the same time. "I'll drive," he said.

"I beg your pardon?" Shelley said in a voice that would have frozen anyone else.

"I said I'll drive. I'm not riding with no broad."

"Bobby, dear—" Phyllis bleated.

But Shelley didn't need help. She gave Bobby her look, which had been known to make car repairmen and school principals cringe. "This 'broad' owns the vehicle and pays the insurance. You'll ride with me, or you'll walk."

"Oh, dear—" Phyllis said.

Bobby opened the back door, nearly yanking it off the hinges, and threw himself in next to Phyllis. Shelley climbed into the driver's seat with frigid dignity. Her knuckles on the steering wheel were white. Before pulling into traffic, she jammed a Christmas music tape into the tape player with a savage gesture.

Jane lit another cigarette.

Everyone pretended interest in traffic. They were two miles from the airport before anyone ventured to speak.

Phyllis, her voice a bit shaky, said, over the sounds of "It Came Upon a Midnight Clear," "Oh, look. It's starting to snow. How wonderful. You can't imagine how I've missed snow all these years. And how I've missed Chicago. Not that I don't love living on the island—but I always get a little sad at Christmas. Chet has a pine tree flown in from Canada every year, of course, but it's not the same when you're sitting around in shorts with the windows open. A pine tree just doesn't smell the same in a warm climate."

"Screw the snow," Bobby mumbled.

"Oh, now, Bobby darling! You can't fool me," Phyllis said with ponderous jollity. "You're happy to be back. You'd miss a Chicago Christmas as much as I have."

"There's nothing about Chicago I'd miss."

"Are you from Chicago?" Jane asked him, desperate to get the conversation on a friendlier footing.

This wasn't the way to do it.

"You mean Phyl didn't tell you all about Mommy's Little Bastard?" he asked.

"Bobby, I've told you that you mustn't say things like that," Phyllis said.

"Why not? It's the truth."

"Phyllis, I was telling Shelley about the beautiful Christmas ornaments you made when we lived in that apartment—" Jane broke in frantically. "Remember the one with the starched lace you gave me? I still have it."

"You don't! Oh, Jane, how sweet of you."

"You'll have to show me how you did it. We're putting together a church bazaar right now, and we need all the help we can get. Maybe we can run over to the craft store after you've unpacked—"

"Oh, I'd *love* that!" Phyllis said. "A Christmas bazaar! You can't know how much I miss such things. We live such an isolated life on the island.'' She paused, perhaps sensing that she was wandering right back into the same territory Jane was trying to save her from. "Yes, I think I remember how to do those ornaments. Tatting, wasn't it?"

"Maybe you can show my daughter, Katie, how to tat. I'm hopeless, but she's pretty good at that sort of thing," Jane said.

"Is that knitting you have in your bag there?" Phyllis asked.

"Crocheting, actually. Is that knitting you have along with you?"

"Just some little hats and mittens I'm making for charity. It gives me something to do with my hands. And I'm working on a sweater for Bobby, too. A sort of crimson; his color, I think."

Bobby had sunk into some silent reverie of his own. He was glaring out the window at the snow as if he could stop it by sheer disapproval. Shelley was no longer driving as if she were looking for a cliff to plunge them all over. The rest of the ride home was taken up with pleasant talk about crafts. Jane dragged out her afghan and showed it to Phyllis, who admired it enormously and reciprocated by hauling forth an elaborately designed sweater.

Eventually Jane started breathing normally, but in the back of her mind, she was turning over the problem of what to do about her guests. Phyllis apparently believed that the invitation to visit was open-ended. Jane supposed a month-long visit wasn't odd at all in the lifestyle Phyllis was accustomed to. After all, if you had a whole hotel to put your guests up in, they could stay for years without being a nuisance. Jane was certain Phyllis had no idea she was being an imposition.

A month with Phyllis—with any stranger underfoot in the house—would be bad enough. But a month with Bobby Bryant? Impossible. Within a week somebody, most likely Jane herself, would kill that boy.

Shelley, who smirked and said nothing, or a summer

— 4 —

Shelley pulled into Jane's driveway. She unlocked and
opened the back doors of the minivan, then stood aside
and watched while Jane and Phyllis sorted suitcases
from church bazaar cartons and unloaded the luggage.
"I don't suppose it's crossed *your* mind to help?" Shelley said to Bobby, who smirked and said nothing.

Overhearing this, Jane handed him a suitcase with
such force that it nearly knocked his breath out. "We've
got it all sorted out. You can carry them in now,
Bobby."

"What an adorable house, Jane!" Phyllis said.

"Thanks, Phyllis," Jane said, miffed. "Adorable"
had cute, cosy connotations to her. As if it were merely
a summer cottage. Well, from Phyllis's viewpoint, it
probably was. She reminded herself that Phyllis had
meant it well.

"Here, let me help you with those, Bobby!" Phyllis
was saying. Jane was tempted to break her arm.

Shelley was closing the sliding side door, and Jane
went to get her bag of crocheting off the floor of the
front seat. "Shelley, I can't tell you how sorry I am—"
she said quietly.

"Jane, my dear, you're going to be much sorrier before you get rid of them. I don't know who I dislike
most—Bobby for being such a jerk or your friend, Phyllis, for not knowing it."

"Do you think she doesn't know? Or is she just not willing to admit it?"

"The subtleties don't interest me. Whatever it is, it comes to the same thing in my book," Shelley said.

"I'm really sorry—"

Shelley softened. "I shouldn't be a bitch to you. It's just that I haven't been so mad in years. He really is a bastard, regardless of birth. The status can be earned, as well. But it's not your fault. You had no idea what was coming."

"What *am* I going to do with them?"

"We'll get rid of them somehow. Trust me. Just don't let that boy near me again."

"Thanks for driving. Please don't abandon me now."

"Jane, you saw me through having my wisdom teeth extracted while my mother-in-law was visiting. That's a moral debt I intend to clear up this week."

They joined Phyllis and Bobby, who had gathered all their luggage—a substantial pile of fantastically expensive leatherwork—at the kitchen door next to the driveway. Phyllis and Bobby were in the midst of an argument. Or at least Bobby was treating it as such. "I can't be stuck here with no wheels, Phyl."

"Of course you can't, darling. I'll call a car rental right away."

"I don't want some old fogy kind of car. I want something sporty to take back to the old neighborhood."

"Oh, Bobby, do you really think you should—?"

"You gonna tie some rope on me or something?"

"Of course not, darling. You know I wouldn't interfere in what you want to do. I just don't think it's wise to—"

She stopped as Jane forced her way between them to unlock the kitchen door. She decided that if Phyllis wanted to haul suitcases around when there was an able-bodied young man on hand, she could do so, but Jane Jeffry had too much sense. She strolled into the kitchen and held the door open. Shelley managed to be right on her heels, unencumbered with so much as an ounce of Phyllis or Bobby's luggage.

"Come out, Willard, it's not burglars," Jane called, as Phyllis and Bobby wrestled suitcases. A moment later the big dog emerged timidly from behind the door to the living room. He was wagging his tail in a craven manner as if to suggest that he was merely waiting to be absolutely certain of the evidence before attacking.

"I think if burglars actually came in here, he'd probably read them their rights," Jane said with disgust as Willard shambled up and sniffed Phyllis's feet. "There's also an army of cats around someplace. Max and Meow will turn up when you least expect them."

"What a dear doggie! I haven't petted an animal for years," Phyllis said, bending to stroke him. "Chet has terrible allergies, poor man. He knows how much I love animals, so he's always buying the most adorable stuffed animals for me. There's this shop in Paris that sends a man every year with samples. Isn't that amazing? The man has to miss days of work to fly down to the island. I think it's so sweet of him."

"Phyl, the car—" Bobby said.

Just for a second Phyllis looked at him as if she'd never seen him before but then got her doting look back. "Jane, do you have a phone book around?"

"Yes, I'll get it while you're unpacking."

"Phyl, now," Bobby said.

"Surely you can wait a few minutes and let your mother get settled," Jane said in the tone she used with the kids in the car pool who were misbehaving. Out of the corner of her eye, she noticed that Shelley, who couldn't even bring herself to spank her poodle to make him behave, had balled up her fists as if to pummel someone momentarily.

"No, Jane. It's fine. I'll just give them a quick call," Phyllis said.

Jane handed her the yellow pages and sat down at the kitchen table. She wanted to put her head in her hands and weep. Phyllis had never been one of the world's great brains, but could she possibly be this stupid? The poor man from the toy store missed days of work flying from Paris? Why, Chet Wagner must have put in a couple thousand just getting him there. And to buy a grown woman expensive stuffed animals?

Jane tried to remember Chet and could only come up with a dim impression of an older man (not so old, really, probably only the age Jane was now) with a worried expression when Phyllis wasn't around and a euphoric one when she was. He must have really loved her all these years with an uncritical, unquestioning love. Proof of what love could do without a brain. But Chet wasn't a stupid man. You don't buy whole islands on the profits of stupidity. However, if the relationship had been successful in the past, what made it stop working now? Jane was torn between curiosity and the fear that Phyllis was going to explain it all to her—at length.

And what did Chet think of Bobby? More important, what did he think of the way Phyllis knuckled under to the overgrown brat? Surely Chet wouldn't approve. Or did Chet automatically accept anything Phyllis did or wanted? The loathsome Bobby had to be at the heart of the trouble, but hadn't Phyllis said that it was Chet who dug up Bobby? What an odd marriage.

Bobby had wandered into the living room with Willard trailing him. Phyllis covered the mouthpiece of the phone and whispered to Jane, "Is a Jag a fancy car?"

"Very fancy. Go for it, Phyllis," Jane said, hoping

her old friend didn't hear the unwitting sarcasm in her voice. Thank God Shelley had wandered off to the guest bathroom and hadn't heard the exchange. She'd have probably grabbed Phyllis by the hair and beat her head against the wall. Or at least she'd have looked like she wanted to. Where had Phyllis, who didn't even know what Jaguars were, found a place that rented them? Phyllis's ways were mysterious indeed.

"They're bringing it over in a minute, darling," she called to Bobby when she hung up.

"Phyllis, I'm putting you in the guest room at the end of the hall upstairs. Bobby can take your bags up there," Jane said loudly enough that the boy would hear. She wondered if maybe the neighbors could hear, too. "Bobby'll have to sleep on the sofa bed in the basement."

"Oh, no. Let Bobby have the guest room. I'll be fine in the basement," Phyllis said.

Jane dug her heels in. "No. Impossible. Bobby, take your mother's things upstairs."

Phyllis smiled. "I guess we mothers always think of the children first, don't we?"

Shelley, now back from the bathroom, made a noise somewhere between a snort of outrage and the beginning of a coughing spasm.

Jane was amazed that anyone could utter such a remark without choking on it. "I don't see why we should, Phyllis. Kids are much more resilient than we are. My Mike could sleep on a pile of rocks and not notice. Come on up, and I'll show you your room and the bathroom and everything." Hesitant to leave Shelley alone with Bobby for fear of what she might do to him without supervision, Jane reluctantly took Phyllis upstairs, all the while fighting the desire to apologize for the accommodations.

The "guest room" was really a sort of accidental cubbyhole she usually used for storing cartons (all of which were now "stored" in her own bedroom). It had a double bed, a chair, a tiny dressing table, and a closet the size you might find in a train compartment. Worse, Phyllis would have to share a bathroom with Jane's kids, a gruesome fate.

But Phyllis didn't find anything odd or inconvenient about the arrangement. She admired the pretty bedspread, commented favorably on the view of the field behind the house from the small single window, and complimented Jane on the felt Christmas banner hanging on the wall over the bed.

"Phyllis, I hate to be rude, but there's an errand Shelley and I have to do. I promised to help her take some things out of her car, and I don't want to stick her with the job. It'll only take fifteen minutes or so. Do you mind if I leave you here to unpack?"

"Of course not," Phyllis said, giving her a quick hug to emphasize her sincerity. "I don't want to be the least trouble to you."

"You're no trouble at all. I'm glad to have you here," Jane lied. And yet, it wasn't entirely a lie. If it hadn't been for Bobby, she'd be enjoying Phyllis's presence.

Bobby was blitzing through television channels, try-ing to find something to suit his tastes when Jane came back down. Shelley was in the kitchen, pacing. "Bobby, I'm going to run an errand," Jane called. "When I get back, I'll make up your room in the basement. I'll only be gone a little while."

He kept pushing the buttons on the remote control until he finally found MTV. Then he turned up the volume. If he'd been one of her children and ignored her, Jane would have snapped the set off, but he wasn't hers—thank God!

Shelley was out the door and had started the van before Jane could even climb in. They rode in silence, the magnitude of Jane's plight having overwhelmed them both. Once Jane whimpered a little, and Shelley patted her hand.

Shelley pulled into the curved, hedge-bordered drive of Fiona Howard's house. The construction of this home in Jane and Shelley's neighborhood had caused some-thing of a stir a few years earlier. A conflagration (started by a grease fire caused by a notoriously bad cook and taken as a sort of divine culinary retribution) had seriously damaged two adjoining homes as well. The central house, as well as the two neighboring ones, were purchased by a couple named Fiona and Albert Howard who, to everyone's surprise, made no attempt to repair the damaged homes to the side. Instead, they leveled both of them, as well as the middle one, and built a new house on the triple lot.

This was considered an extravagant thing to do, but surprise had turned to disappointment and a certain measure of animosity when, before construction was even completed, a visually impenetrable wall of hedges went in around the entire site. Worse, the owners were seldom around during the construction process, so there was almost no opportunity to get to know them or their floor plan. This thwarting of natural nosiness was considered very unfriendly.

The mystery of the Howards' apparent secretiveness was solved, however, a scant week before they moved in. The realtor let drop an historical reference that was picked up and picked apart. The elusive Mrs. Howard, it turned out, was the former wife of Richie Divine, the late rock star whose untimely death had shaken the country—or at least the female half of it—as badly as Elvis Presley's.

Known to keep a public profile so low as to be nearly invisible, Fiona Howard was an extremely unwilling celebrity, almost a legend in a slightly pejorative sense. This made the hedge practically acceptable. After a while neighbors started to take a certain pride in it. "Oh, that hedge?" they would say to visitors who were taken blocks out of their way to "happen" to drive past. "Why, that's the Howard estate—Richie Divine's widow, you know."

It was Jane's first time behind the hedge.

"Jane, help me with these boxes," Shelley said, opening the side door of the minivan.

Jane got out and braced herself to lift a particularly large carton. She nearly threw it over her shoulder when she gave a mighty heave. "Dear Lord, is this empty?"

"No, it's those embroidered Santa pillows the Parslow sisters made."

"Oh, dear—" Jane had seen the prototype pillow last summer and had been appalled. The rosy-cheeked Santa had looked like a lecherous old alcoholic. The stitching that was meant to give him a rosy nose looked like broken veins, and to make it worse, he was leering horribly.

As they reached the front door, it opened, and Fiona Howard came out to meet them. "Shelley, Jane," Fiona said warmly in a lovely upper-class English accent that made Jane feel she'd stepped into the middle of a Masterpiece Theater production. "I didn't hear you drive up. Here, let me help with those. I can call Albert to help us if you have anything heavy."

"No, we can manage. Just point me in the right direction," Jane said over the top of the Santa pillow carton.

"Just down the hall, then. I'll have the maid help me unpack them later."

"We'll come back and do that," Shelley said, staggering under the weight of a box of iced gingerbread men. "You're not supposed to go to any trouble, since you're letting us use your house for the sale."

"I don't mind in the least. But can't you stay?"

Jane had set her carton down and come back. "Not this morning. I have an old neighbor coming to town to stay a few days." Even saying it made her shudder. "I left her at home unpacking. If it's okay, we'll come back tomorrow and help you sort things out."

"Can't you even have a cup of tea?" Fiona asked.

"That nice jasmine kind?" Jane asked.

"If you like."

Jane shot a questioning look at Shelley, who glanced at her watch and said, "Only for five minutes. I have to be at school pretty soon to help the nurse weigh the third graders. Some sort of health unit.''

Fiona led them through the house, and Jane dawdled as much as she could, looking around. She knew Fiona only slightly from church, and she'd never been within the hedged walls, much less inside the house before. She'd expected it to be palatial. Actually, it was quite ordinary, but in a very expensive, tasteful way. The only Englishness about it was the formal living room, which was done with a busy patterned carpet that was probably eighty dollars a yard minimum, imported. The room was furnished in elegant, dark furniture that was certainly antique. The rest of the rooms they passed were just what any well-to-do American family might have. Jane was sorry there wasn't linen-fold paneling and ancestral portraits hung from picture molding.

Fiona led them to a small, sunny breakfast room that overlooked the backyard and spacious garden, dormant now but obviously well tended. Fiona and Shelley fell into a discussion of the proper packaging and pricing of some hard candies that would be for sale at the church bazaar, and Jane studied Fiona.

She, unlike her home, was satisfyingly English. Her hair was a burnished copper and the tiniest bit curly. It might even fuzz on a humid day. Her skin was as fair as milk and her eyes almost neon blue. She must have been a striking girl and was still attractive, but she had a bit of middle-age hippiness starting, and there were a few gray hairs in with the red. The large white teeth that must have made a ravishing smile in youth were the tiniest bit horsy at thirty-five. She looked like Fergie, the Duchess of York, would probably look like in a few years.

"You don't know anyone looking for a house, do you?" Fiona asked, as she poured three cups of fragrant tea.

"You're not selling, are you?" Shelley asked.

"Heavens, no! We wouldn't dream of leaving. It's the house next door to the north. The lady who lived there has gone into a nursing home, and her son is trying to sell the house. He explained to Albert about some tax thing or another that makes it imperative to sell it before the end of the year. I think he might price it quite reasonably. It's only two bedrooms, I believe, but for a single person or young couple it would be ideal."

"Single? Do we know anybody single, Jane?" Shelley asked with a smile. "I hardly remember the state."

"The only single people I know are divorced with mobs of kids. Like myself."

"I didn't know you were divorced, Jane," Fiona said, passing her an elegant china sugar bowl.

"I put that badly. I'm not. I meant I'm a single parent with mobs of kids. I'm a widow."

"Oh, I'm so sorry. I had no idea. How tactless of me," Fiona said, a genuine blush of embarrassment brightening her cheeks.

Jane almost smiled. How odd that Fiona, a rather famous widow herself, should apologize to Jane. "Please, don't be sorry. It's been nearly a year now, and I'm quite accustomed to it—" Jane stopped. "Listen to me! I'm already picking up your accent. That's a terrible habit. I don't mean to do it."

"Jane grew up all over the world, and she tends to talk like whoever she's talking to," Shelley explained. "Even if it's just a speech impediment, she mimics it."

"I never!"

"You certainly do. Remember that woman in the grocery store last week who couldn't say her 'r's? She asked you where the sausages were, and you said, 'Wight down the thiwd aisle.' "

"I didn't."

Fiona smiled and said, "Still, if you hear of anyone needing a small house, give me a call. We're uneasy about it standing empty. One hates to have an invitation to vandalism so close, you know."

Shelley asked, "Doesn't that Finch man live on the other side of it?"

Fiona looked as if she'd been caught in something. "Yes, he does. But I really believe he's harmless."

"Harmless! I wouldn't call anybody who poisons dogs harmless," Shelley said.

"There's no proof it was Mr. Finch," Fiona said. Her voice lacked conviction. "We've never had any trouble with him."

Jane had been so interested in listening to Fiona's accent that she'd hardly started on her tea when Shelley started bustling her along. "Fiona, we'll be back tomorrow to help with setting up. Please don't go to any trouble on your own."

"Please feel free to bring your houseguest along if she's interested in helping out," Fiona said to Jane. There was something vaguely poignant in her voice. Loneliness? No, that couldn't be, Jane thought. You can't be rich and famous and lonely.

As they reached the front entry, a man stepped into the area from another door. "Oh, Fiona, I didn't know you had guests."

"Albert, this is Shelley Nowack and Jane Jeffry. They're on the placement committee for the church bazaar."

"How nice to meet you, ladies," Albert Howard said. He was American—a plumpish man with thinning dull brown hair and oversized tortoiseshell bifocals that made his receding chin appear almost nonexistent. Fiona had taken his arm in an oddly protective gesture and was gazing at him as if he'd just spoken words of enormous import.

"We've met before, I think," Jane said. "I substituted for Mary Ebert in the church choir one morning. You were there."

Albert stared at her for a minute, recognition dawning, then started to laugh. "Oh, yes! The director ended up asking you if you'd just hum."

"I didn't expect you to remember the occasion in detail!" Jane said. "My enthusiasm for music slightly exceeds my talents."

"Jane—?" Shelley said with a meaningful glance at her watch.

"Odd, aren't they?" Shelley said as they pulled out of the driveway moments later.

"You're a mind reader," Jane said, smiling. "I had no idea he was Albert Howard. I see him in the church choir, but I never connected him with Fiona. How could she have married him?"

"He's a very nice man, I hear from people who know him. Very soft-spoken and witty."

"Yes, but married to Richie Divine's widow? I mean—Richie Divine was so—"

"Sexy?" Shelley asked.

"Slim, young, blond, talented, gorgeous, famous, rich, I was going to say. But I guess sexy sums it up. Was he really, Shelley, or were our hormones just at fever pitch when we were young and he was alive?"

"There's evidence against it," Shelley said, craning her neck around to peer at traffic behind her. She changed lanes in such a way as to nearly cause a beer truck to run onto the shoulder.

"What evidence?"

"Well, there's the fact that my mother and her friends thought he was wonderful, and none of them were much given to admiring young men. Mostly their impulse was to bat them around the ears for impertinence. Then, too, there's that old movie he was in—I saw it on the late show a month or so ago and found my tongue hanging out."

"Can you imagine slobbering over Albert Howard after having been married to Richie Divine?"

"No, but apparently Fiona can. You're sounding like the press. Remember the flap when it was revealed that Richie'd been married—?"

"Of course! Who could forget? Every girl in America thought she'd been personally jilted."

"And then the reporters just about crucified Fiona when she remarried. As if it was really anybody's business."

"I'd forgotten that, but I can see why. It's sort of like an ex-president running for county dogcatcher."

They were silent for a few moments, then Jane spoke again. "It makes me sad. If I'd been married to Richie Divine, I'd have never considered remarriage."

"Stay a widow, forever worshiping at the shrine? Is that how you feel about your husband?"

"Lord, no! But Steve was hardly Richie Divine."

"Maybe Richie Divine wasn't either."

"What in the world does that mean?"

"I'm not sure," Shelley said. "It's just that he might not have been so 'divine' to live with. To be young and idolized might have made him an egotistical bastard at home. It would have been odd if it didn't. And it can't be fun living in the glare of public scrutiny—bodyguards everywhere, not being able to just run to the mall and shop or do anything like a normal person. You remember last year when Paul had that convention of his franchisers?"

"Yes?"

"Well, I got a little taste of very minor celebrity at the convention. Everybody was either toadying to me or resenting me because I was the boss's wife. It was creepy. I can see how Fiona's glad to be out of it.''

"I guess so, but why pick somebody like Albert Howard, the ultimate nerd?''

"Maybe he's terrific in bed,'' Shelley speculated.

"Hmmmm—'' Jane was sorry the subject had come up. Her imagination in such matters, after nearly a year of widowhood and celibacy, was beginning to revive like a desert plant suddenly watered.

"Forget hormones,'' Shelley advised. "Let's figure out how to get rid of your houseguests.''

—— 6 ——

It was too short a ride to come up with any clear plan. They discussed and discarded murder, arson, bribery, rumors of epidemic, and outright rudeness. Shelley dropped Jane at the sidewalk and tore off to fulfill her school obligation.

Jane had just gotten in the house when the Jaguar was delivered. Jane was amazed at the way things worked for Phyllis. Perhaps there was something in her credit card number that tipped merchants off that they'd hooked a big one. The man who delivered the car all but swept off a cape and offered to let her walk on it.

Within minutes of the car's delivery, Bobby was gone, without apology, explanation, or indication of his anticipated return schedule. Phyllis gave him a handful of money and watched him screech away. A sickeningly fond look remained on her face long after he disappeared. Jane thought the odds were pretty good that he'd wreck the Jag by evening.

Phyllis went to her room to finish unpacking. Jane noticed that it was only one o'clock. This had already seemed a very long day, and it wasn't half done yet. She sat down at the kitchen table and smoked another cigarette. How many was that today? Far too many. What *was* she going to do with these people?

"Are you hungry?" she asked Phyllis when she came down from her room. She'd changed into jeans and a plaid shirt with a red sweater over it. Common enough outfit, but the jeans were so perfectly fit and faded that Jane was certain they'd cost a fortune, and the sweater was probably hand knit from certifiably virgin Scottish sheep.

"Starving," Phyllis answered.

Jane grabbed a package of lunch meat, a head of lettuce, and some mayonnaise from the refrigerator and pulled out a loaf of whole wheat bread that didn't have any green fuzzy spots on it yet. Phyllis, who was probably accustomed to meals that cost as much as Jane's car was worth, fell to making a lunch meat sandwich as if it were gourmet stuff. Jane reflected that while Phyllis could be irritating, there was still a streak of enduring innocence in her that had drawn Jane to her so many years ago. She suspected that Phyllis really didn't recognize a difference between pâté de foie gras and plastic packaged lunch meat.

Jane smiled. How must Chet have felt all these years about handing the world on a silver platter to a woman who would have been happy with Melmac?

"Well, I guess you're dying to know all about Bobby?" Phyllis asked as they sat down to eat.

Jane wanted to say she'd rather have a Pap smear than know anything more about Bobby, but courtesy won out. "Yes, tell me everything."

"Everything" about Bobby turned out to be mercifully concise. According to Phyllis, she and a high school classmate had run off to get married when she was only fifteen and he a year and a half older. Both sets of parents went after them and three days later dragged them back to Philadelphia. The annulment mechanism was put into action, and in no time, the marriage was as if it had never been.

Except that Phyllis was pregnant.

Her parents arranged for her to go to Chicago and live with her aunt until the baby was born and could be put up for adoption. That duly accomplished, Phyllis had stayed on in Chicago to take a secretarial course, partly because she got along far better with her aunt than she ever had with her parents. She was working as a secretary when she met Chet Wagner, married him, and lived happily ever after.

"What about the boy? The one you married? Did he know about the baby?"

"Heavens, no!" Phyllis said. "I wanted to tell him at first. I was really happy about it. Then I thought it over. My parents *made* me think it over. I may not be brilliant, but I was smart enough to see how relieved he'd been when the marriage was annulled. And I couldn't blame him. It wasn't as if we were madly in love or anything. In fact, we'd only had two or three dates when we ran off together. We only did it, I think, because we were both unhappy at home, and that seemed a way out."

Jane felt this didn't ring quite true. The part about the boy being relieved might be so, but Phyllis sounded like she'd probably been crushed by the knowledge that he'd been glad to be free of her. Had this version—not really in love, just wanting out—come to her then, or was it the product of long years of thought and reflection? Jane was astonished to learn that Phyllis had actually undergone such emotional upheaval. "Didn't you regret that it didn't work out?" she asked.

"No, if I'd stayed married to him, I'd have never met Chet. I liked him—the boy I ran off with—maybe even loved him, but we were too different. He was real smart, you see. Ambitious and all that, too. He'd have gotten tired of me. Chet's smart and ambitious, too, but in a different kind of way. I don't know quite how to explain it."

In spite of herself, Jane was fascinated. She wished Phyllis were more articulate. "Did you ever see the boy you married again?"

Phyllis paused, as if trying to remember. After a moment she said, "We never met again. I didn't go back home except once or twice, and he moved away as soon as he finished high school."

Jane suddenly had a devastating sense of exactly what they were talking about. The Phyllis who ran away and got married was about the same age as Jane's daughter, Katie, and the boy had been the age of her son Mike. Katie and Mike were *babies*! Yes, Jane would probably have done just what Phyllis's parents had done—break it up, put the baby up for adoption, and let the kids have another chance at life.

To cover an involuntary shudder, Jane got up and fetched a bag of potato chips and a plastic carton of dip. "So what about Bobby?" she asked when she sat back down. "How did you find him—and why?"

"Well, I'd never told a soul about having a baby. Not even Chet. It was the only secret I had from him, and it always bothered me. Then, about a year ago, Chet was out on the ocean in his boat, and there was a terrible storm. While I was waiting for word, I realized that if Chet died, I'd have that secret on my conscience forever. So when he got back safe and sound, I told him about having Bobby. I mean, about the baby. I didn't know his name was Bobby."

"How'd Chet take it?"

"Oh, Jane, I was so afraid he'd be disgusted with me, but he was wonderful. He knew how sorry I was that we'd never had children. He said that he had his sons and I should at least get to know mine. He got some person who worked for him to find Bobby—"

Some person who worked for him, Jane reflected. That's how the rich did things. Wonderful, thoughtful

Chet buying Phyllis yet another new stuffed toy. Only this one could bite and make messes in their lives.

"Bobby's adoptive mother had died, and his father remarried someone who just couldn't get along with poor Bobby, so they were happy to let him come visit us on the island. And we all got along so well that he stayed with me."

I'll bet he did, Jane thought. Having driven some poor stepmother crazy, he was suddenly thrown into incredible wealth and a brand new mother who worshiped him. What young man wouldn't have stayed? Bobby might be pond scum, but even pond scum knew when it was onto a good thing.

"Jane, I can't tell you what a comfort it's been to have Bobby these last few months. Without him to lean on, I'd have probably just gone to pieces. You see, Chet has been acting very strange. It isn't anything Bobby says or does, exactly, that's so comforting. It's just knowing I have him. Somebody who is my own. Chet's boys are very nice, but they were half-grown before I got to know them, and they're so—so businesslike. Not like Bobby at all."

Oh, Bobby's businesslike enough, Jane thought bitterly. He's gotten into a lovely investment, and he knows it. Too bad he doesn't know enough to treat it with the respect it deserves. "What does Chet think of Bobby?" she asked.

"He loves him!" Phyllis said with almost shrill confidence. "He doesn't really understand him, but he loves him."

"Doesn't understand him how?" Jane felt she shouldn't be picking at this, but she wanted some confirmation that Chet wasn't as foolish as Phyllis.

"Oh, just little things. Chet's a very affectionate, very open person, and he's just a little disappointed that Bobby's so—so reserved."

Disappointed that Bobby's a sullen jerk who treats you like shit, Jane thought. Well, good for old Chet. "What about Chet's sons? What do they think of Bobby?"

"Everett lives in London and handles all the European part of the business. He's never met Bobby, but John—Oh, Jane, you must know John and Joannie, don't you?"

"I don't think so, but Shelley does."

"That's good. I mentioned you to John, and he said he knew you. Something about a ball game. Basketball? Volleyball?"

"Oh, *that* John Wagner!" Jane suddenly remembered him. Boy, did she ever remember him! She and Steve had belonged to a neighborhood volleyball team for a mercifully short time the autumn before Steve died. John Wagner, the captain of the team, was a good-looking, athletic man in his mid-forties who played volleyball as if the future of the human race depended on the outcome of each game. He was a Type-A personality run amok. People had told her he was quite nice if one didn't presume to engage him in competition of any sort, but she'd never believed it.

Jane had looked forward to the first game, buying a cute, sporty outfit and new sneakers. Her game plan had been to stand around looking smashing while other people yelled cheerful things like, "Heads up" and "I've got it." But John Wagner had disabused her of this concept within the first five minutes. His remarks to her had included, "If I'd known you couldn't hit an elephant in a closet, I'd have gotten that ball," and "You've never heard of spiking, then?" and "If you'd quit carrying on like that it would stop hurting."

She never went back, and Steve lasted only three more weeks before coming home in a rage, muttering about neighborhood bullies.

John Wagner and Bobby Bryant trussed up together by family ties was impossible to imagine. "Yes, it was volleyball," she said to Phyllis and, refraining from rubbing her hands together in glee, asked, "How does John like Bobby?"

Phyllis looked troubled. "It's odd, Jane. They don't get along at all. John was quite rude to Bobby both times they met. I suppose it's jealousy. All men are just grown-up boys, aren't they?"

"Jealousy? Of what?"

"Chet's affection, of course."

Or Chet's money, Jane thought. As Phyllis's son, Bobby might have a financial claim on her and, therefore, on Chet. John Wagner wasn't a model person, but it wasn't unreasonable that he might fear and dislike Bobby even more than most people would.

Aside from Phyllis, did the boy have a friend in the world?

Sooner or later, she was going to have to hear about Phyllis's marital problems, so she decided to get it over with. Jane asked, "Why didn't Chet come with you to Chicago?"

Phyllis paused a long time before she answered. "I— I really don't know. I thought it would be wonderful to have a good old-fashioned Christmas here—a nice dinner with John and Joannie and all Bobby's adopted family. But Chet never liked the idea. I kept bringing it up, and I guess it irritated him, because he finally said—"

She stopped, as if choking on the next words. With a sort of funny hiccup, she suddenly got up and ran to the guest bathroom. Before Jane could figure out what to do, Phyllis came back, dabbing at her eyes with a folded piece of toilet paper. "I'm so sorry to act silly, Jane. I want to tell you the truth and get it over with, but it's so hard for me to say. You see, Chet finally said

I should just take Bobby and go to Chicago—forever, if I wanted.''

She started sniffling into the toilet paper. ''I didn't want that. Not in a million years, but he kept insisting, and then one day I had a terrible headache—not that that's a good reason—and I snapped back and said I'd be glad to go away from him. I didn't mean it, Jane. You know I didn't mean it. But the next morning, Chet was gone. He'd flown off on a business trip without even letting me say I was sorry. On the bedside table were two one-way plane tickets and a checkbook. Jane, I should have just torn them up, but I got mad instead. And after that—I don't know. It just got worse. Bobby even tried to find Chet to talk to him and explain that we didn't want to leave—''

''I'll bet he did,'' Jane said, thinking what a shock it must have been for greedy Bobby to find he was about to be cut out of a life he'd just discovered suited him so well. ''I mean—''

But Phyllis had accepted the remark at face value and plowed on, still sniffling. ''I've seen things on television about men having middle-age problems. Male menopause, I think they call it, although I think that's a peculiar term. Still, I think that's what Chet must be going through. I know he didn't really want me to leave, but I did go so that he'd have the time and freedom to rethink our marriage. He's just being irrational. I'm praying he'll come to his senses. We've had the most perfect marriage in the world, and nothing's changed, but Chet has turned into a different person for no reason.''

''Phyllis, there *has* been a change. Bobby.''

''But that's a change for the good!'' Phyllis insisted. ''Chet is crazy about Bobby. He offered to send him to college or on a nice long trip to Switzerland for the skiing—''

—*Anything to get him out of his hair,* Jane thought. Surely even Phyllis couldn't fail to see the truth in this. And yet, it was amazing what people could fail to see if they put their minds in it, she realized with a sick feeling. She herself had managed to be completely blind to her own husband having an affair right under her nose. When Steve had announced that he was leaving her, it had been a hideous shock. She'd never suspected, and even if someone had tried to tip her off in advance, she probably would have refused to believe it. Just like Phyllis was working so hard at not understanding the trouble.

Should she try to make Phyllis see? There were so few really good marriages in the world, and it was a terrible pity to see one sacrificed on an altar as unworthy as Bobby Bryant.

"Phyllis, let me ask you something—what if you had to choose between Bobby and Chet?"

"Jane! What a terrible thing to think of. Why would I have to choose?"

"I don't know, but suppose you did."

"Why, I'd stay with Bobby, of course. As much as I love Chet, Bobby needs me more. A man can have many wives, but a boy only has one mother. You know that. You wouldn't abandon your children for anybody."

"But my children are young. Bobby's an adult, and he's managed without you all these years," Jane said, knowing she might as well try to reason with a geranium.

"He's still my baby. My only baby—" Phyllis said, making another dash for the bathroom.

I can't do her any good, Jane thought with a sense of sadness so profound it brought tears to her eyes.

The phone rang, cutting the conversation short. Jane picked it up with relief. Even somebody trying to sell her bronzed baby shoes would be a welcome break. But it wasn't a salesman, it was Fiona Howard.

"Jane, I hate to disturb you, but I have a bit of a problem. I didn't realize that Albert had scheduled the exterminators to come this afternoon, and I'm worried about any food that might be in some of these bazaar boxes. I know about the gingerbread men and the hard candies, but several people have dropped things off since you were by here this morning, and some of the cartons appear to have different things in them. I'm afraid there could be something in the bottom of one that we might be poisoning. I know Shelley isn't available to help, but I want to have all the food items safely out of the house before they start spraying—"

"I'll run over and see if I can figure out what's what," Jane offered. Phyllis had come out of the bathroom again and seemed to have a grip on herself. She was puttering around, cleaning off the kitchen table.

"I hate asking you when you have company," Fiona was saying. "I tried to ring Shelley first, just in case she'd changed her plans, but there's no answer at her house. Do bring your friend along, and I'll make us a lovely tea. No, I guess I can't even do *that* with the bug people here."

"We'd love to come, tea or not. We could all go out for Cokes at McDonald's."

She hung up and told Phyllis. "I've got to run over to a neighbor's house and take care of a crisis with the church craft bazaar. You don't need to come along if you'd rather rest, but I'd be glad to have you. We can talk more about this later," she added, knowing there was little else she could say.

"Jane, we don't need to talk about me anymore. I just felt I owed it to you to explain. You have problems enough, I'm sure, without mine. I'd love to help if I can," she said. The way her face lit up, it was obvious that she was sincere. As she mopped her eyes a final time, she said, "Chet's so sweet and generous, and I don't ever mean to sound ungrateful, but if there's anything I've missed all these years, it's that sort of thing—church bazaars, other women who like crafts and things. Of course, a lot of real artists used to come to the island, but they weren't interested in things like Christmas ornaments and knitting and Easter egg decorations."

Jane had a sudden vision of Phyllis fluttering around a modern-day Picasso, trying to interest him in styrofoam wreaths.

"I read about this wonderful thing you do with Easter eggs that makes them look batiked. I'm dying to try it," Phyllis went on.

"I think Fiona does that. You can ask her about it."

"This Fiona isn't Fiona Howard, is she?"

"Why, yes. Do you know her?"

"No, but we know some people who know her, and they mentioned once that she lived in the same suburb as you do. You can't have many neighbors named Fiona. Such a pretty name."

"Then you must know who she is—"

"Richie Divine's widow. Yes. That was so terrible

the way the newspapers and magazines were so mean to her when she got married again. I'd like to meet her, and I really want to help with your bazaar.'' As she spoke, she was putting the leftover food in the refrigerator.

Jane suddenly felt a great wave of guilt for not liking her better. Silly as Phyllis might be, she was also very sweet and down-to-earth. There was something innately good about a woman who probably hadn't so much as lifted a dirty dish in fifteen years, but who pitched right in, clearing the table without a second's hesitation. There were good reasons Chet Wagner had stuck with her for so long. If only Phyllis could see the one excellent reason he got fed up.

Jane was quiet all the way to Fiona's house, mentally chastising herself. Wasn't part of the reason she got irritated with Phyllis a matter of simple jealousy? She'd mentally accused John Wagner of being jealous over money, but maybe she was, too. After all, Phyllis was an extraordinarily wealthy woman. Jane, who wasn't exactly poor, still had to carefully monitor every penny. Steve's life insurance and his share of the family-owned drugstores had left her with enough money to comfortably afford the necessities and a precious few of the less expensive luxuries. But while Phyllis was ordering up a Jag for Bobby to drive around without even needing to ask what it cost, Jane was driving a four-year-old station wagon and would have to drive it to death—either its or hers.

Was it Phyllis's money that was getting under Jane's skin? Jane thought not. Lots of people had more money than Jane did. Almost everyone she knew, in fact, either had more or lived as though they did. And she'd never been particularly aware of resentment before. Fiona Howard, for instance, was certainly in a financial class with Phyllis. She must have been her husband's heir, and Richie Divine records were still played on the radio all the time. Just last summer Jane had bought a tape of his old stuff. They hadn't had children, so all the royalties must be going to Fiona. And yet, Jane had never felt jealous of Fiona, only mildly curious about how she lived.

For that matter, the Nowacks were absolutely loaded, but she never felt jealous of Shelley. Shelley's husband had started and owned a nationwide Greek fast-food franchise that was nearly as common nationally as any of the hamburger or pizza places. But Shelley still bought her sneakers at K Mart and saved grocery store coupons and was always complaining about telephone bills. Of course, if Shelley had been renting a car, as Phyllis did a short time ago, Shelley would have found out the price of everything on the lot and would have demanded a discount if the tires had more than a thousand miles on them.

No, it wasn't a matter of money or lack of it. It was a basic difference in mentality or outlook or something that made Phyllis rub Jane the wrong way. No point in analyzing it, Jane told herself as she steered the old station wagon into the Howards' hedge-lined drive. Phyllis and her hideous son would be out of her life pretty soon, and she wouldn't need to worry about it. In a day or two, she'd just have to tell Phyllis in the nicest way possible that they were going to have to move into a hotel. And if she couldn't find a nice way—well, she'd worry about that later.

Fiona met them in the driveway. "Jane, I've been calling, but I missed you. I'm so sorry I put you to this trouble. Just after we hung up, the exterminators called and said their truck broke down, and they won't be here until tomorrow. I've dragged you out for nothing."

"It's fine. It still has to be done by tomorrow, and we might as well do it now. Fiona, this is my friend

Phyllis Wagner, who's visiting me—for a few days," she added. "Phyllis, Fiona Howard."

The two women greeted each other, subtly summing each other up as women do. A flickering glance to assess hair, clothes, manners, then—recognizing they were nominally equals—the warmth of tentative acceptance passed between them. "Fiona, you and Phyllis have some friends in common."

"Oh? Who is that?"

Phyllis looked confused. "I'm not sure. I mean, I told Jane I knew about you living here because someone mentioned it, and I recognized the name of the suburb because of Jane. But I can't remember who it was."

"What a pity. Where are you from?"

"Originally Philadelphia, then Chicago. But for the last thirteen years, my husband and I have been living on a little island in the Caribbean."

She made it sound like she had a Quonset hut on somebody else's beach.

"Phyllis and her husband own the island and the hotel on it," Jane couldn't resist saying.

Anybody else might have goggled at this; Fiona was unmoved. "How interesting that must be," she said with friendly blandness. "I've always liked the Caribbean, but I can't stay there long, because I sunburn so badly. Albert and I went to Jamaica once, and I got a horrible burn, in spite of the fact that I slathered on so much suntan lotion I couldn't sit on a chair without sliding off. Do you miss the seasonal changes?"

This, of course, was one of Phyllis's favorite topics and elaborations took them into the house and into the ground floor guest room where the church bazaar cartons were stored. Jane studied the array of boxes for a moment, wondering where to start. They were stacked everywhere with only a narrow aisle between them.

Fiona had said a few people had dropped things off since this morning, but it looked more like an army had looted a small, holiday-oriented country and left all the spoils here.

As Jane stood, gazing with bewilderment, she heard Phyllis saying, ". . . And it will be so nice to be back permanently."

"Back permanently?" Jane asked, roused from her stupor by these chilling words.

"Yes, I was telling Fiona about moving back. We haven't had time to talk about it yet, Jane. Chet told me to find a nice house here, and he'd buy it for Bobby and me if I wanted."

"You're going to live in Chicago?" Jane tried to sound bright and cheerful but felt like she had a mouthful of mud. Having Bobby Bryant around permanently would be about as much fun as having a car wreck in a Pinto. She had to suppress the urge to run to the nearest phone, call Shelley, and scream, "Help me! Help me!"

"Maybe you'd be interested in the house next door?" Fiona asked, obviously as a conversational gambit, not as a sincere suggestion. "I was telling Jane about it just this morning." She went on to explain chattily about the old lady, the nursing home, and the son's anxiety to get a tax break by selling before the end of the year.

"That might be very nice," Phyllis said. "At least it would give me time to look around for something else without imposing on Jane. And we'd be so close. Wouldn't that be fun, Jane? Just like the old days."

Please don't do this to me, God. I'm a good person, and I don't deserve it, Jane thought.

— 8 —

Jane held up a pinecone wreath and pretended she hadn't heard the question. "I wonder who made this. It's awfully nice work, isn't it? It's got these little peppermint sticks woven in, but they're not meant to be eaten anyway—"

"Would you really like to take a look?" Fiona was asking. "The man left us a key in case I wanted to show it to anyone."

"That would be fun, but we should help Jane—"

"Why don't I have Albert run over with you, while I—"

"Did I hear my name being taken in vain?" Albert had apparently come down the hallway just as Fiona referred to him.

"Oh, Albert—you know Jane Jeffry, she was here earlier. And this is her friend Phyllis Wagner," Fiona said.

He looked at Phyllis, at Jane, and at the room full of cartons and was struck dumb.

"It's not as chaotic as it looks," Jane assured him. The man had actually paled at the sight of what had happened to his home. "I pretty well know what all this stuff is, and it'll be out of your house in another week or so, after the sale."

Fiona explained to Albert, who still looked stricken, what she wanted him to do, but he obviously didn't want to be bothered acting as somebody else's real estate agent. "I'm expecting the accountant any minute. He's bringing some forms over that need to go in by midnight."

"I'll keep him entertained if he shows up," his wife assured him. "It'll only take you a minute."

"But Fiona—"

Jane glanced up, aware of the tension growing in the room. Albert was on the verge of digging his heels in. Phyllis was looking at him with undisguised fascination, as if he were some sort of museum exhibit: "The Nerd Who Married Richie Divine's Widow." Jane suddenly understood why Phyllis couldn't think of the name of the friend they had in common. There wasn't such a person. Phyllis had just kept up with the fan magazines and had been curious about Fiona and her husband.

Too bad Albert was such a loser, physically—the little pot belly, the thinning dull hair, the jowls that drew attention to his almost complete lack of chin. Everybody must look at him and make the comparison between Fiona's current husband and her former husband and wonder what on earth she saw in this one. It couldn't be easy to be Albert Howard.

"If you'd just let me in, I could take a little look around and bring the key back?" Phyllis suggested.

"Good idea," Fiona agreed.

"Oh, very well, I'll take you over there," Albert replied. It was just short of openly hostile. "Come along, Mrs.—uh—"

"Wagner, but you must call me Phyllis," she said, following his rather abrupt departure from the room. "I'm just sorry my son isn't with me. He's looking forward to coming back to Chicago, I think. He was raised here. You see—" Her voice stopped as a door closed. Good Lord, Jane thought, she's telling *him* the whole story. The woman didn't know the meaning of discretion.

Fiona started sorting boxes with Jane but seemed preoccupied. "Albert seems to be a bit out of sorts," she finally said. "It must be something about the accountant. I think, too, that he worries about anybody having to live next door to Mr. Finch, but after all, somebody has to. The township can't just level the whole block. I don't think he's half as bad as people say, do you? At least, he might not be. We had an old lady in the village where I grew up that everybody claimed was a witch, and she was really a sweet old thing when you got to know her. She just had an intimidating manner. Jane, what *is* this stuff?"

"Oh, that! It was a gorgeous angel-hair angel that Suzie Williams made, but it's sort of turned into a blob with a head. Max and Meow got into it before I brought the carton over. I'll just pretend to have bought it before the sale starts so we don't have to put it out. Here's the box with the fruitcakes. Where shall we put the things with food?"

"Just out in the hallway. I'll have the maid move them to the family room, and then the yard man can take them out the back door to store in my car until the bug people are gone."

Jane smiled. "You know, I heard once that there are only a hundred fruitcakes in existence. Every year everyone exchanges the same hundred, and nobody knows they're the same ones."

"I can believe that. My family had a fruitcake that was an heirloom. We kept giving it to my Uncle Charles, and he kept giving it back on alternate years. I think he eventually sold it to an antique dealer," Fiona said with a giggle.

"So about these—there's no point in three people

moving them. Just point me toward the family room, and we'll eliminate one stage of the process.''

Fiona gave her directions, and Jane staggered out. The family room turned out to be the most interesting—and strange—room of the house. It wasn't really a family room in the usual sense. It was more of a shrine. The walls were adorned with all Richie Divine's gold and platinum records. Jane had never seen a real gold record in her life, and she walked around the room looking at them, awed. Completely apart from their meaning, they were beautiful things in a flashy way.

There was "Red Christmas," the sappy but moving ballad about two young lovers separated by the Berlin Wall. Jane remembered hearing once that three of the biggest selling Christmas records year in and year out were Elvis's "Blue Christmas," Bing Crosby's "White Christmas," and Richie Divine's "Red Christmas." The commentator liked the irony of the three dead artists with the patriotic color scheme outselling so many of the live ones.

Next to it was the platinum disk of "Good-bye, Philly," the heartbreakingly lilting little song that was released, with terrible irony, the same week Richie died. The song had stayed on the charts for months and months afterward. It had a sort of "You Can't Go Home Again" theme, adapted to the seventies.

Katie had been an infant when that came out, and Jane always associated the song with sitting in the kitchen, listening to the radio, and waiting for the bottle sterilizer to finish boiling. That had been such a happy, peaceful time for Jane. Life had been so simple then. And yet Fiona, at the same time, was enduring the heartbreak of losing her sexy, famous husband. It was hard to believe that anyone could have been unhappy at the same time Jane was so contented.

Jane didn't remember the words to the song, but she

could still hum the whole thing, and she did so as she continued her tour of the room. There were platinum records for "Do I, Do I Ever," "Some of These Nights," "Everything I Am," and at least a dozen more. Jane stopped in front of "Loving Loving You," and came close to blushing. Steve had bought her that record the day they came back from their honeymoon.

On a shelf that ran along the north wall there were ranks of other awards and framed pictures. Richie with Bob Hope in fatigues entertaining troops someplace. Richie with President Nixon. Richie with a frumpy middle-aged couple who must have been his parents. Richie with a couple astronauts and another of him in a silly mock embrace with Elizabeth Taylor. There were three shots of Richie receiving awards and four stills from the one movie he'd made. A big color poster advertising the movie hung in the center.

At the end of the wall, almost lost in the shadows of the corner were two charming photos. One was a strip of four pictures taken in a drugstore booth. Richie and a very young, pretty Fiona. In the top shot, he was making a face, and she was looking at him with shy amusement. In the second, he was nuzzling her neck, and she was looking mortified. The third was a serious face-forward shot of both, and in the last they were kissing primly. How sad it must make her to see that now: Richie, his youth preserved by death, and Fiona, growing steadily older. She already looked old enough to be the mother of the boy in that shot. Why did she keep that reminder of what she'd lost?

The other photo at the end of the shelf was a shot of what must have been a high school band lined up on the school steps. Someone had circled a boy at the end wearing an oversized hat and holding a big drum. His face shadowed, you'd never recognize him, but that must have been Richie. Jane studied the picture, feeling she'd seen it before—the cheerleaders with their pom-poms kneeling in the front, the band director standing at the side, the kids squinting into the sun, the boy on the back row holding two fingers up behind the head of a girl in front of him. Every high school band picture in the world must look just like that.

Jane had lost all track of what she was supposed to be doing and was brought back to reality with a start when Phyllis's voice broke in on her thoughts. "Jane, where are you? Have you seen that house? It's darling. Just darling! I'm sure Bobby is going to love it."

Jane hurried out of the room, afraid Phyllis would find her there and gush over the Richie Divine memorabilia. She wasn't sure why she didn't want Phyllis to see that room, but she didn't. She felt so sorry for Albert having to share his house with his extraordinary marital predecessor. Of course, Albert was presumably living on the spoils of his predecessor's talent, so apparently it didn't bother him.

The rest of them, including Albert, had gathered in the sunny breakfast room. Whatever had irked him must have passed, because he was sitting at the table, looking utterly relaxed.

"It has this sweet little porch off the main bedroom with a little railing. Wonderful for sunbathing," Phyllis gushed.

"She nearly toppled off, admiring the view," Albert added.

"Could I use your phone to call and make arrangements?" Phyllis asked.

"Certainly, but what kind of arrangements?" Fiona asked, setting a tea kettle on the stove.

"To buy it," Phyllis said. "Would you write down the address and the name and number of the man who's selling it?"

"Yes, of course. But don't you think you're acting just a little precipitously?" Fiona asked.

"I probably am," Phyllis agreed cheerfully, taking the business card Fiona had handed to her. She went to the phone.

"Did Albert tell you about Mr. Finch?" Fiona asked, apparently overcome with an urge to be fair.

"He mentioned him, yes. But he just sounds like an unhappy old soul to me. I'm sure I'll get along with him just fine." Without another word, she dialed and said, "Mr. Whitman, please. George? Phyllis Wagner here. Yes, lovely trip. George? I've found the most adorable house I want to buy. Would you contact this man—" She gave the information and waited impatiently while he wrote it down.

"Now, it's vacant, and I'd like to get in immediately. Tonight? Why not? What's a closing? Oh, I see. Then ask him if I can just rent it until then. And George, it's quite empty now. Could you please send a decorator over this afternoon with a few things—beds, linens, kitchen things, towels, you know—so I can move in tonight? Yes, I know you will, George."

Jane listened to this with fascination. Could you just buy a house and move in six hours later without even knowing what a closing was? She'd never heard of such a thing. And she heard it now with mixed feelings. On the one hand, it was wonderful to think she might not have to harbor Bobby under her roof for a single night. Too good to be true. On the other hand, it installed Bobby and Phyllis in her own neighborhood on a more or less permanent basis. Besides her own concerns with this possibility, she hated to do that to Fiona. She was a nice lady who didn't really deserve to get stuck with Bobby as a next-door neighbor.

But Fiona had started it by mentioning the vacant house, Jane told herself. It was really her own fault, and who could tell—maybe they'd all get along great. She glanced at the Howards. Fiona was looking gracious and English and seemed to be drifting gently from slight worry to puzzlement and back. Albert, however, was gazing out at the frozen garden, stirring his tea and humming to himself. Phyllis, temporarily restored to her usual cheerfulness, had the phone receiver pressed to her ear and was gabbing away at her Mr. Whitman about the house.

Jane mentally shrugged. *Whatever happens, it won't have anything to do with me,* she thought.

She was seriously mistaken.

—— 9 ——

On the drive back home, Jane mentally prepared herself for the ordeal of helping Phyllis get her new home ready. To her astonishment, Phyllis didn't seem inclined to do anything nor, as it turned out, did she need to. During the afternoon there were two calls from a man who politely introduced himself as Mr. Whitman of Wagner Enterprises asking for Mrs. Wagner. The first time, Jane slipped out of the room to throw in a load of wash. The conversation was over when she came back up, and Phyllis made no reference to it. The second time, Phyllis took down a couple of phone numbers, thanked Mr. Whitman, said yes, she usually did prefer yellow to blue, then hung up.

Jane had the uneasy sense that someplace people were having nervous breakdowns and tearing their hair out in a desperate effort to please Phyllis, who was blissfully working on knitting a crimson sweater for Bobby.

"I heard once that Queen Victoria could sit down anytime she wanted without looking back to see if there was a chair behind her," Jane said as she dragged out her own afghan to attack.

"How odd. Didn't she ever fall down on the floor?"

"No. That's the point. There were people around her whose job it was to anticipate her every wish and be ready for it."

"What a strange way that would be to live," Phyllis said. "Whatever made you think of it?"

Jane stared at her for a moment, wondering madly whether she could possibly fail to see the parallel. Apparently she could, and did. "I don't know. It just ran through my mind. Phyllis, do you really think you're doing the right thing to buy that house without even considering it or talking it over with Chet?"

"Oh, but I have considered it, Jane. You see, I don't believe it's over between Chet and me, but I might be wrong. I came here meaning to stay as long as necessary." Her chin was trembling again, but she plowed on. "And if I'm right and he wants me back, having my own home will show him that I'm coming back out of choice, not because I don't have anywhere to go or know how to take care of myself. If we can reconcile, it will be better if I have this house. And if we can't— or it takes a while for him to come to his senses, I'll have a home."

In a weird way, she was making sense. Except that her self-reliance so far had consisted of calling an employee of Chet's and asking him to make all her arrangements. "But Phyllis, why here?"

"Because Chicago is where I feel at home."

"Don't you like living on the island?"

Phyllis put down her knitting, picked up a corner of the afghan Jane was working on, and looked it over as she spoke. "I never thought about it. I guess I didn't like it or dislike it. It was just where we lived. As long as I was with Chet I would have been content at the North Pole. Where you live really doesn't make the least difference, you know. It's what you are that matters."

Jane—who had grown up as a State Department brat and had lived such diverse places as Saudi Arabia, Washington, D.C., England, Brazil, and Norway—

disagreed utterly but realized it would be pointless to argue that point. She supposed if you discounted climate, wildlife, geography, religion, politics, and local customs, all places *were* pretty much the same. You had to have Phyllis's mentality to fail to notice such differences, however.

Jane couldn't let herself get distracted from the subject at hand. "What I meant was, don't you think you'd stand a better chance of patching things up with Chet if you stayed on the island instead of so far away?"

"I don't think so. He'll miss me a bit, and the farther away I am, the more he'll miss me. At least I hope so. And he can always just resell this house I've bought."

Jane suddenly realized she was applying her own standards to the wrong person. Buying a house was a once-in-a-lifetime event to her. To people with the money and staff the Wagners had, it was no more significant than checking into a motel. A temporary thing.

"I've got to pick the kids up in a few minutes," she told Phyllis, resolved not to worry about the disparity between their financial statuses anymore. "You're welcome to ride along, but you'd have to be crazy to volunteer. This close to Christmas they're so hyped up it's like riding in a car with a herd of frenzied gazelles."

"Thanks, no," Phyllis said with a laugh. Then she became instantly serious. "Jane, I so wish I'd had what you have."

"What on earth is that?"

"Oh, driving children to school. That sort of thing. I missed all of Bobby's growing up. I wish I could have picked him and his little friends up from school."

It was more than Jane could stand.

"Phyllis, that's the sappiest thing I've ever heard! You have no idea what you're saying. The school parking lot is the deadliest place in the world. There's always one pea-brained woman who parks blocking the drive and goes off and leaves her car. And then there's usually at least two boys who walk past the line of cars running their hands—and sometimes a sharp object—along the sides of the car. No matter how carefully you investigate the children, you end up with one in every car pool who's never ready in time—''

''Investigate the children?''

''Oh, sure. Getting into a car pool is like applying for high-level government security clearance, except it's done more subtly. From preschool on, each child and his driving parent are accumulating a performance record. Before you allow a new person in the car pool you have to know all about their past. Does the mother take her fair share of driving without whining? Can the kid be controlled in the car? Do they live on a street that has good snow removal in the winter? With older kids, you have to take into consideration such things as whether a girl is given to wearing too much perfume— that can be deadly in a closed car—or whether the kid plays a very large band instrument. That's what counts against me, and I know it. Even when you check all that out, once a week somebody goes home with some-one else without bothering to pass word along to that day's driver, and you have to comb the school building for them. They leave their books, their mittens, and their half-chewed bubble gum in the backseat. Occa-sionally they throw up their breakfast on the way to school. One of my girls last year managed to get her hair tangled up in the door handle, and I had to cut her loose. Her mother was furious and sent me a bill from the hairdresser for fixing up the damage.''

Phyllis was laughing and wiping tears from her eyes. ''Aren't there *any* good things about driving the chil-dren?''

''Oh, yes. There's one. When a woman has her hands on the wheel of a moving car, she's perceived as part of the mechanism. She ceases to be a mother, or even a human being with ears. The kids will say anything. Things they'd sooner die than tell you, they'll talk about endlessly in a moving car. It's the only way I have any idea what my children are up to. Phyllis, I've got to get going. Help yourself to anything you want if you're hungry. I'm fixing spaghetti for dinner. You aren't allergic or anything, are you?''

"Not to anything and I love spaghetti. Say, Jane— George Whitman said Chet's son John has been trying to get hold of me. Something about the business, I think. Not that I know anything about it. But would you mind if I invited him to come over here to talk to me? Not for dinner, of course—''

"I wouldn't mind a bit," Jane said mendaciously. *Just so long as he doesn't bring along a volleyball,* she was tempted to add. "There are some cookies in that jar you can give him. I'll only be forty minutes or so.''

Shelley was just coming in her driveway as Jane got ready to go. Jane went over to Shelley's car window. "Is there anything I can do to make up to you for this morning? Kiss your feet? Give you my firstborn?''

"You give me one more kid and I *will* get even. After I lined the little darlings up to be weighed, I had to be the reading lady for the third graders. The usual volunteer was sick. Sick, my eye! The canny bitch was just smarter than me. They were climbing me like a jungle gym. Why don't they all have nervous breakdowns before Christmas? More to the point, why don't we? Think it over, Jane. It's not a bad idea. We could stage some sort of seizure in the front yard. Foam at the mouth and chew sticks. They'd take us off to a nice sanitarium where somebody else has to wrap the gifts and stuff the clammy turkey and get hives taking the vile tree down when it's over.''

Jane considered. "Doesn't sound bad. Do we get to wear our jammies all day?"

"Sure. If we play our cards right, we might even talk somebody out of wheelchairs, and we wouldn't even have to walk anyplace."

"Would our families be able to visit us?"

"I certainly hope not!"

"It wouldn't work for me. My mother-in-law, Thelma, would take over my kids."

"So let her. It would serve her right."

"Yeah, but she'd convince them of her theory—that I was really a pathetic slut their father married out of pity."

"Well?"

Jane laughed. "Gotta go. Anything I can do for you while I'm out?"

"Nothing. Oh, yes. I'm trying to fix that gingerbread house that got the corner smashed. I'm out of powdered sugar."

"I've got some. Just help yourself."

"And go in your house? With your company? Have you lost your mind?"

"Bobby's gone. Only Phyllis is there." At the sight of Shelley's raised eyebrows, she added, "I'll buy you sugar. Say, Shelley, do you know John and Joannie Wagner?"

"You already asked me that this morning. I've been thinking about it. I know *a* Joannie Wagner. She and I are putting on the P.T.A. tea next week. You know her, too. She's the one who made all those grapevine wreaths for the bazaar. Hard-working, lovely voice, and very pleasant but dumpy, defeated looking."

Jane understood this to apply to Joannie, not the wreaths. Now that she'd been reminded of who she was, she thought about Joannie Wagner as she headed toward the junior high. Jane knew her very slightly and had never made the connection between her and Phyllis or even between her and the aggressive volleyball player she was married to. Poor Joannie Wagner *was* a beaten-down sort of woman. Her hair was always curled, but badly. Her makeup was never quite right somehow. She wore expensive, but ill-fitting clothing and gave the general impression of a scared rabbit. Of course, she was a rabbit. What else could you be if you were married to John Wagner? You'd have to have the stamina of an Amazon and the temperament of a wolverine to assert yourself around a man like that.

She hoped Phyllis wouldn't be able to find him to invite him over. The last thing Jane needed was John Wagner in her house. If only she could go back to when she stupidly made that halfhearted invitation to Phyllis to visit. But as she pulled into the school parking lot she realized that, even knowing what was in store, she'd have probably done the same thing. Phyllis and Company might not be any fun, but Phyllis needed a friend and considered Jane to be one.

——10——

It was a rare and treasured morning that Jane didn't have to drive at least one school car pool. Even when her schedule wasn't thrown off by something like the electricity going out, with three children going to three separate schools that started at three different times, it took planning worthy of General Motors to work out a system that left her free to slop around in robe and slippers on an occasional morning.

This was such a morning. Jane had risen earlier than usual to get a head start on putting out the Christmas decorations. She got out the crèche and set it up on the table just inside the living room doorway. She dragged some greenery in from the garage where it had been waiting, encased in plastic and sprinkled with water, for two days. Draping it along the mantel above the fireplace, she then dug through the Christmas storage boxes until she found the string of twinkle lights she wanted. She put the traditional red tablecloth on the dining room table and set out her collection of Santas from around the world on the sideboard.

Unfortunately, that was all the further she'd gotten by the time she had to get the kids stirring. Now she leaned on the kitchen counter watching the driveway for Mike's ride to arrive. Mike, her high schooler, was in the middle of the kitchen floor trying to force a tuba into its elephantine case. He was mumbling angrily, and Jane was being very careful not the hear the exact words. If she did, she'd have to be motherly about his language, and he was under enough pressure already.

"You wouldn't think a tuba could actually grow overnight, would you?" Jane said, trying to cheer him up.

Mike looked up at her and said scathingly, "Mom, do you realize if I can't get this thing to fit, you'll have to drive me? I can't make everybody wait."

Jane abandoned cheerfulness. "I don't see why not. I wait nearly every morning I drive for Scott to finish combing his hair. Cram the thing in. I'm *not* driving anybody anywhere today."

"You could let me have the car," he suggested.

"Not if you set my hair on fire."

"That's not fair, letting him have the car," Katie said, galloping down the stairs with Jane's purse in her hand. "Can I have five dollars?"

"What for, and I'm not letting Mike drive, and what difference would it make to you if I did?"

Katie ignored all but the first of this. "The ninth-grade field trip to the Art Institute. You said I didn't have to pay school things out of my allowance."

"Agreed, but how can it cost five dollars to ride a school bus to town?"

"Mother, there's lunch," she explained condescendingly.

"Take five. Not a penny more. Mike, your ride is honking. Todd, what did you do with the skin?" she added, noting that her fifth grader had cut up a banana into his cereal, and there was no sign of its original container.

"I dunno," he said, tearing his gaze away from the cartoons on the kitchen television long enough to glance around the table and his lap.

Jane had been vaguely aware of thumping and thrashing in the living room for some minutes and went around the corner to look. As she feared, Willard was there, tossing the banana skin around with a puppyish abandon that ill became a grown dog. "Willard, give me that thing!" she shouted, lunging at him just as he flipped the banana skin up onto the half-finished afghan. This dislodged an indignant Meow, who had been curled there, happily milk-treading the soft yarn.

"Pets are supposed to lower your blood pressure," Jane complained to no one in particular as she stuffed the banana skin down the disposal. "My blood pressure is about to blow the top of my head off. Katie—are you ready? Did Mike leave?" she added to Todd. He didn't reply, but the tuba and case were gone, so the eldest must have left.

Katie was shaking some Rice Chex into her hand—and a few on the floor that Willard was inhaling. "What happened to your friend, Mom? Wasn't she supposed to stay here? You made us clean our rooms and everything."

"No, she stayed in the house I told you about. If you'd come home for dinner instead of staying at Jenny's, you'd have known all about it. And in the future, when you're going home with Jenny, you have to tell me in advance."

Katie ignored all the references to her transgression the afternoon before. "You mean she just bought a house just like that? Neat. Denise Nowack said her mom said your friend's son was really cool looking. You should have kept him here."

"That was fair-minded of her. I assume Mrs. Nowack must have also mentioned that he's a creep."

"Yeah, but that's mom-talk," she said, stuffing another handful of cereal into her mouth. "Can we go over tonight so I can meet him?"

"Not if I can help it. Isn't that Jenny's mother honking?"

Katie flew past, her backpack full of books catching the milk carton at the edge of the counter. It bounced on the floor and shot a white geyser across the room. "Sorry—" Katie's voice was cut off by the door closing behind her.

The phone rang. If that was somebody asking her to drive Todd's group, she was going to pretend they had the wrong number. "Yes?" she said cautiously into the receiver.

"Jane, this is Fiona. I'm sorry to call so early, and I hope I'm not alarming you unduly, but there's something going on next door. The house your friend moved into last night—"

"What kind of something?"

"Well, there's a police car over there, and an ambulance just drove up. I heard some teenage voices late last night. You don't suppose something's happened to her son, do you?"

"Oh, my God! I'll run right over. Thanks, Fiona."

Jane ran into the little bathroom off the kitchen, grabbed a big towel, and threw it at the milk on the floor. It had formed a lake, and Willard and both cats were standing at the shore, lapping.

"What's wrong, Mom?" Todd asked between slurps of cereal.

"I don't know. I think my friend who came to visit yesterday is sick. I've got to run over there. If your ride isn't here by the time I'm dressed, I'll wait with you."

"Oh, Mom. You don't have to. I'm *not* a baby!"

"No, but you're *my* baby, kiddo," she said, ruffling his hair as she ran by.

Upstairs, she kicked off her slippers and slithered out of her robe and T-shirt style nightgown and flung herself into underwear, jeans, and a red, hooded sweatshirt. A glance in the bathroom mirror confirmed her fear that adequate cosmetic help would take too long—

possibly days. She looked like she'd been left out in bad weather overnight. She made do with a quick smear of lipstick and a swipe at her hair with a hairbrush. She heard a faint "Bye, Mom," and the slamming of the kitchen door as she was putting on her boots.

She ran down the steps, grabbed her mystery-fur jacket from the front hall closet, and started looking for her purse. Where would Katie have left it? Ah, next to the refrigerator. She was hampered by the fact that Willard and the cats were pacing around the kitchen in the happy anticipation of being fed now that the kids were gone. "You've got to wait, guys," she told them as she flew out the door.

By the time she got to Phyllis's new home, there were three police cars, plus the ambulance, and a familiar red MG. Damn! That was Mel VanDyne's car, and she looked like the dog's dinner. Someone had strung a thin yellow plastic banner across the front yard that said, "Police Line—Do Not Cross."

Jane got out of the car and paused to get her breath. It wasn't easy. Her heart was racing, and she was feeling sick. Police line—Detective VanDyne—ambulance. Something terrible must have happened to that horrid Bobby Bryant. Had he invited some of his former friends from the city to his mom's new house and gotten beaten up? Or had he already had a run-in with Mr. Finch next door? Poor Phyllis. As much as Jane disliked Bobby, she hated for Phyllis to be unhappy, and Phyllis would be miserable if something had happened to her darling.

Stepping over the yellow strip, she went to the house, aware of the multitude of other neighbors peering from front windows up and down the street. An officer was just coming out of the front door as she approached. "Lady, do you live here?"

"No, but a friend of mine does."

He leaned back inside the door. "Hey, Mel, there's somebody here who knows these people."

Mel VanDyne came to the door, took one look at Jane, and said, "Oh, no."

Not precisely the reaction she would have liked from a man she was planning to invite to Christmas dinner. She had met the handsome (and somewhat younger) detective a few months earlier when he was investigating a murder. Jane herself had been instrumental in catching the murderer.

VanDyne had called her assistance "damned dangerous meddling."

Jane had called it "solving the case."

But along the way, Jane had decided that when she was ready to throw herself back into the world of dating, she'd throw herself in Mel VanDyne's direction first. As yet, she hadn't gotten the nerve or the opportunity. Now here she was, frayed and bedraggled, and he was greeting her with "Oh, no."

"Mrs. Jeffry, do you really know these people?"

Jane bristled. "I wouldn't be butting in otherwise. It's my friend Phyllis Wagner and her son, Bobby Bryant."

"Come in, then. But don't touch anything. Just sit down for a few minutes, would you?"

The living room was bare of furniture as yet, but there was a lovely table and six matching chairs in the dining room next to it. A police officer had some forms spread out on the table and was having a cryptic conversation with a walkie-talkie. Jane sat down obediently and waited for Mel, who had gone up the stairs. She ought to go straight to Phyllis to help comfort her, but she knew if she started wandering around the house, Mel would have her head.

As she waited, a medical attendant called down the

stairs to his co-worker, "Bring me that extra blood pressure cuff, would you? This one's sprung a leak."

At least Bobby wasn't dead, if they were taking his blood pressure. Probably not even hurt too badly, judging from the man's tone. Of course, those guys weren't supposed to act hysterical, but he'd sounded downright casual. The other attendant went back to the ambulance and then upstairs. A moment later, both of them came down carrying a stretcher.

The body on it was completely covered.

Jane looked away quickly. Poor, poor Phyllis! To have found her long lost son, only to lose him. What in the world had happened to him?

Mel came back down the stairs carrying a little book of some sort. He pulled up another chair and said, "Could you look through this address book and tell me who ought to be notified of the death?"

"It was an accident, wasn't it?" Jane asked.

Mel cocked an eyebrow. "I don't normally get sent out when people slip in the bathtub or fall off ladders. No, it was no accident. It was murder. I'm sorry, Mrs. Jeffry. Are these people good friends of yours?"

"Not really. I'd never heard of Bobby until yesterday, and I hadn't seen Phyllis for fifteen or sixteen years. Poor Phyllis. How's she doing?"

"I beg your pardon?"

"How's she taking it?"

Mel paused a moment, then to Jane's astonishment, he took her hand. "I guess you'd say she's taking it badly. She was murdered."

—11—

"Phyllis—murdered!" Jane gasped.

"I'm afraid so," Mel VanDyne said, withdrawing his hand, which she'd clutched so hard his fingers hurt. "Why did you assume otherwise?"

"I don't know. But—but—how? Why? Who?"

"That's what I hope you might help me find out. That is," he put up his hand in a "stop" gesture, "help me *just a little.*"

Jane was still too stunned to understand the implication. "Where's Bobby, then?"

"Upstairs. Recovering. He's about half drunk and half hung over and he's been violent. Fell over trying to attack one of my men, and hit his head on the door frame. He'll be okay. Why did you think he was the one who'd died?"

"Just because he's so horrible, I guess. Do you have a cigarette?" He handed her one and lit it for her. "I'm trying to quit," she said, exhaling. "Fiona Howard called me. She seemed to think it was Bobby. Who in the world would want to kill Phyllis? She never hurt anybody in her life. This is awful."

"We'll find out. Don't worry. Now, you can help by telling me about her. What was she doing here? The local police have this house listed as vacant. They've been keeping an eye on it periodically to prevent a break-in."

80

"It was vacant, until last night." She drew a deep breath, trying to compress an explanation of who Phyllis was into as few words as possible. Among Mel VanDyne's traits was a certain tendency to regard Jane's explanations as wordy and full of trivialities. "Phyllis and I knew each other seventeen years ago—"

"Seventeen years—?" he said brokenly, as if expecting a day by day accounting of the entire duration.

Pruning it to the minimum, she got the story out.

"Now, let me get this straight," Mel said after he'd thought for a few minutes. "Mrs. Wagner and her husband have no children together, but he has two sons from a previous marriage, and she had one she'd given up for adoption: this Bobby Bryant. Where's her husband?"

"I'm not sure. Possibly on the island where they live, but he wasn't there when she left. She told me that. He could be anywhere in the world. He has international business interests. You don't think he had something to do with this?"

"I'm not thinking anything. Just asking questions."

"Come on, that sounds like a line from 'Dragnet.' "

He smiled. "Just where I learned it. You like it?" He went to the kitchen and returned with a saucer for Jane to use as an ashtray. "Tell me about Mrs. Wagner. What was she like?"

"I don't know, really."

"But you said she was coming to stay with you for Christmas."

"No, she was going to try to. But I was determined it wasn't going to happen when I'd met Bobby. As it was, she didn't stay with me at all. We went over to help Fiona Howard—the big house on the triple lot next door—with something, and Fiona mentioned that this house was for sale, and Phyllis bought it. It was Fiona who saw you over here and called me."

"Yesterday? She got here yesterday, saw a house, bought it, and moved in—all in the same day? That sounds like something from *Willy Wonka.*"

"I know it does. I thought so while it was happening. I don't know that she'd actually bought it yet, but she called some man to take care of it, and she met him and her husband's son John over here to sign some papers around six o'clock last night. Maybe she just signed a letter of intent and a rental agreement. I don't know. I wasn't with her. I just gave her my car to use while I was fixing dinner."

"So she moved in then?"

"No, she came back and had dinner with us, and I brought her back over about nine—after some people delivered furniture and bedding and stuff."

"People with furniture. She sees the house, buys it, and gets it mainly furnished in one day? Are you serious about this?"

"I know it's weird. See, Phyllis had been used to having tons of money and just telling people to get things done. And they got done."

"She was overbearing, then?"

"No! Not in the least. It was like she thought that's how everybody lived. She was poor when she married Chet, but she was also very young, and he made lots of money fast. I think she'd just gotten used to living that way and forgot about things like weighing decisions and counting your money and shopping for bargains and waiting for things you want."

Mel was unconvinced. "The way you talk, either she was incredibly stupid or—"

"Or I'm making it up? She wasn't stupid. At least not as stupid as she must seem to you, hearing about her. She was just out of touch with reality. It seemed that Chet Wagner adored her beyond belief. He took her off to his own little fantasy world. They didn't have television, and she was never much for reading, so it was easy for her to get out of touch with real life. I don't think she ever consciously realized she was rich.''

"Come on!"

"I mean it. I don't think she ever assessed much of anything. She hadn't many introspective brain cells. Yesterday when I asked her things about Bobby and Chet's relationship, she looked like it was a totally new concept to her. I honestly don't think she'd ever wondered about it until I asked her.''

"Who was this boy's biological father?''

"I have no idea. Some kid she went to high school with. She told me she never saw him again.''

"She could have lied.''

"No, I don't think she knows how. Oh, dear. That sounds condescending. What I mean is, she could keep a secret, like Bobby's existence, because that meant just not saying anything. It didn't take cunning. But lying would take imagination, and hers was confined to Christmas ornaments and knitting patterns.'' At his questioning expression, she explained about Phyllis's interest in hand crafts. "That's sort of why she was here. At this house, I mean. I'm on the placement committee for the church Christmas craft bazaar—''

"Of course you are,'' he said.

"What does that mean?''

"Nothing at all,'' he said, stifling a smile. "Go on. You're on the placement committee—''

"The bazaar's being held at Fiona's house, and Phyllis came along to help, since she likes craft stuff and is wonderfully creative about it. Fiona told her about this house, and she came over and looked at it, then called somebody—I got the impression he worked for her husband—and asked him to take care of buying it and furnishing it right away. Now I have this awful feeling she was in a rush because she'd caught on that I didn't like her precious Bobby.''

"Didn't she even consult with her husband?''

"No. She was leaving him. Or he'd sent her away. No! Don't get that look on your face! Chet would never have done anything bad to Phyllis. He adored her.''

"You just said he'd thrown her out.''

"It was just going to be temporary. I'm sure of it,'' Jane said, feeling she had to defend Chet, even though she realized how bad this looked for him. "You see, Phyllis was mad about this newfound son of hers, and I don't think Chet could stand him. She didn't say so, but I'm sure that's all that was wrong. My own guess is that Chet figured that Phyllis would see through Bobby sooner if they were off by themselves. And I believe she would have. He was so dreadful—she'd have run out of excuses for him before long. It's just supposition, but I think he probably felt their own marriage would suffer less in the long run if he let her make the inevitable break with Bobby on her own, without his interference. They'd have worked it out. I'm sure.''

VanDyne didn't seem impressed with her reasoning. "So you knew this Chet pretty well, too?''

"No, I hardly knew him at all. I'm just guessing what an intelligent, considerate man would do in these circumstances. I do know that he was both intelligent and considerate.'' VanDyne gave her such a patronizing look that she burst out, "Look, I freely admit I know nothing of police procedure, but I know every bit as much about human nature as you do. Probably more, and I knew these people as well. You didn't.''

VanDyne didn't apologize, but he had the good grace to look properly chastized. "So where was her son all this time yesterday while she was moving in—or having people do it for her?''

Jane felt better for telling him off, however mildly.

"Buzzing around Chicago someplace in a rented Jaguar. We got back from the airport with the two of them around noon, and he was gone half an hour later. I didn't see him again. I imagine Phyllis got in touch with him somehow and told him where to come home. But he wasn't here when I came over with her and her luggage around nine."

"This man she called—who was he?"

"Hmmm, she called him George and asked for a poet—"

Mel VanDyne looked confused. "She called somewhere and asked to speak to a poet? Or she asked George to find her a poet?"

"No, it was a poet's name. Thoreau? Eliot? Chaucer? Defoe? I'll think of it in a minute. He wrote something about lilacs and Lincoln—Whitman, that's what it was. George Whitman."

VanDyne looked up at the ceiling as if despairing of ever understanding her mental processes. "If you don't know where her husband is, I guess we better call this Whitman. Wait, you said her husband has a son or sons in Chicago? What about them?"

"Two sons. One lives in England, I think, and one of them lives around here someplace. His name is John Wagner, but I don't know the street address. I think; on the whole, it would be better to call this Whitman person and let him tell Chet and his sons."

The book VanDyne had brought downstairs was Phyllis's address book. He handed it to her. She opened it and flipped to "W" where there was not only no Whitman, no Wagner, there wasn't anybody. Glancing through, she was saddened to see that fewer than half the letters had any listings. Poor Phyllis really had been isolated. There were two women listed with Philadelphia addresses. Maybe a mother and sister or cousins or something. Working backward quickly, Jane found

John Wagner under "F" for "family" and got clear to "C" before finding Mr. Whitman. He was listed under "Chet's office people."

VanDyne was watching over her shoulder as she looked through the address book. If Phyllis's method of alphabetizing didn't convince him that the woman was out of touch, nothing Jane could tell him would.

"You'll call, won't you?" she asked when she'd finally found Mr. Whitman's number.

He looked at her with wonder. "It isn't a matter of social niceties. It's police procedure."

"Yes, of course. Poor Chet."

While he was gone, making his calls, Jane went upstairs thinking it was only decent to straighten up Phyllis's belongings if the police were through with them. Certainly Chet would want to come get her things. At the top of the stairs, she heard voices from the bedroom at the left, so she turned into the one at the right. She had time for only two impressions before backing out. One, that it was a tiny bedroom, and two, that all that brownish red stuff all over the mattress was Phyllis's blood. It looked like someone had dumped a gallon or so of paint on the bed.

She stood in the hall, leaning against the wall, fighting down nausea, and realizing for the first time that she hadn't even asked how Phyllis had died. She breathed deeply through her nose, trying to fend off the dizziness that was catching up with her. Suddenly someone grabbed her arm.

"What are you doing up here?" Mel VanDyne asked harshly. "You're not passing out, are you? Come here. Clear the way, boys." He dragged Jane through the bedroom opposite the tiny one and yanked open the door to the little deck Phyllis had mentioned. Dragging Jane out into the cold, fresh air, he said, "Take a deep breath. That's it. Good. Another. Now, lean over."

"I'm all right now," Jane said after a moment. "Really. But I'm freezing out here."

He led her back inside. It was a large, airy room with a double bed upon which Bobby Bryant was sprawled with a makeshift cold compress on his head. A burly officer was standing beside him, clearly ready to take care of any further misbehavior Bobby might dream up. Another officer was leaning against the wall just inside the doorway. Jane could see into the pink-tiled master bath next to the cozy sitting room area by the front windows of this room.

"I need an address where I can reach you," Van-Dyne said to Bobby as he got out his pen.

"I'm staying right here." Bobby's voice was slightly slurred and very belligerent. "Old Phyl paid for the place, and now it's mine."

"We'll see about that," Mel said, a muscle knotting in his jaw. Apparently he'd taken just as severe and instant dislike to Bobby as Jane had.

She touched Mel's arm. "I want to tell you something. Downstairs."

He followed her down the steps reluctantly. "He's the sort of individual who makes me long for the good old days of police brutality."

"What's he doing in *that* room?" Jane asked.

"Hell if I know."

"No, listen to me. It's important, I think. If you knew a house had only a tiny little bedroom and a big master suite and was going to be lived in by a single woman and her teenage son, who would you expect to have the little room?"

Mel paused in midpace. "The kid. Yeah—

"Only Phyllis was the kind of sap who let him have the big room. Now, if you'd been a murderer, prowling around in the dark to kill an obnoxious teenager in his sleep, which room—"

"You may have something."

"Something! That's it, and you know it. I kept asking why anybody would want to kill Phyllis. Well, nobody did. They wanted to kill Bobby and got the wrong person in the wrong room. Look, we've only known Bobby a few minutes each, and we'd both adore knocking him off. Imagine how people who knew him better must have felt about him. But Phyllis—nobody could kill Phyllis. Slap her out of sheer exasperation, maybe, but not kill her."

"Possibly."

"You're only saying that because it was my idea. You know that's the solution."

"Good God, woman! Even if you're right, which I'm not admitting, it's not a solution. It's just a line of inquiry."

"That's 'Dragnet' talk again. I'm going home. When you want to know more, you know where I live."

On that victorious note, she marched out the door.

She thought she heard a chuckle just before she slammed the door.

─── 12 ───

Jane got in the station wagon and started the engine but found that she couldn't drive away immediately. Surprise was fading, and shock was setting in. Poor Phyllis was dead. Really and truly dead. In spite of her relatively calm discussion of motives with Mel Van-Dyne, Jane was deeply shaken. Shivering violently and wondering why her hands and feet felt oddly numb, she reached out and turned the car's heating system to high. She didn't trust herself even to drive for a few minutes.

Poor, poor Phyllis.

And the worst of it was, it was a mistake. More than just the enormous moral mistake of any murder; she was a victim by mistake. Jane was sure of it. Nobody could possibly want to kill Phyllis, but practically anyone who'd ever known Bobby would have to fight the impulse. Someone had given up the struggle—and killed Phyllis in error. It was, in a sense, Bobby's fault. It wasn't enough for him to ruin her good, long-standing marriage and make her show herself up as a soft fool. He was responsible for her death, at least secondarily.

Or was it only secondary?

Could Bobby himself be the murderer instead of the intended victim? He was probably capable of it, Jane judged from her slight and very unpleasant acquaintance with him. And he was showing no remorse. He hadn't pretended to give a damn about Phyllis when she was alive and wasn't acting the least bit sorry she was gone. But—

A tap on the window interrupted her train of thought. Swallowing a scream of surprise, she turned to see Mel VanDyne at the car window on the passenger side. She motioned him to get in.

"Are you all right?" he asked, seating himself and twisting sideways to talk. "I shouldn't have let you go like that. I was forgetting that she was your friend. Do you want me to take you home?"

"Thanks, but I'd just have to find a way to get my car back later. I'll be fine in a minute. I needed to sit and think. It isn't that Phyllis was such a terribly good friend, you know—"

Why did she feel she had to be meticulously truthful with him? What difference did it make?

"It's upsetting even when it's a stranger," he admitted. "Very upsetting."

"Then why do you do it? This job?"

He smiled, showing an indentation alongside his mouth that wasn't quite a dimple, but near enough. "To bring evildoers to justice? That's an embarrassing thing to admit. It sounds so unsophisticated, but it's true. Funny. I think you're the first person who ever asked me that. Except for my parents, who said, many times, 'You're going to be *what*?' "

Being truthful sometimes paid dividends, Jane thought. "What will happen now?"

"I've got my men hunting down her husband. We'll question everybody in the neighborhood. We'll check on her background, the kid's, the husband's, the neighbor's, the kid's friends'. All routine stuff to start with."

"Can I help?" Jane asked.

He cocked an eyebrow. He had great eyebrows. Great teeth, too. Jane always noticed people's teeth. His were very white and just irregular enough to give his expression real distinction. And with that 'hint of a dimple that showed so rarely . . .

"I mean some kind of help that you assign and approve of," she said, trying to put aside thoughts of how attractive he was.

"As a matter of fact, you may be able to. I've been thinking about the husband. If, as you say, there was just a temporary rift in the marriage, he's going to take this hard. He's got family and business friends, but he might well want to talk to you, since you spent that last day with her. I don't figure the obnoxious kid will be much comfort. Can you be on hand? To help with funeral arrangements and that sort of thing, if he wants?"

"I'd be pleased to. About Bobby—"

"You're wondering if he killed her himself, aren't you? So am I. Don't worry, Mrs. Jeffry. These things do occur to me."

"Detective VanDyne—couldn't you please call me Jane? It makes me feel very old and frumpy to be called Mrs. Jeffry."

"Sure. I'd like to—Jane. It suits you. I'm Mel."

"Short for Melvin?"

"Even worse. Melton. My mother's maiden name. I've always felt she had a cruel sense of humor."

"Oh, here comes Fiona. She's the neighbor to the south who called me and said you were here. She didn't know it was you, of course, but—"

"I get it." He shifted around and hunted for the door handle. "I'll call you later, Jane.'

"Yes. Thanks. I mean—" What an ass she was being! She wasn't a kid anymore, and he didn't mean he was going to call her for a date or something, for God's sake! He was just going to call in connection with his duties as a detective. Jane felt herself blushing.

He'd stopped, presumably to introduce himself to Fiona, and as he walked back to Phyllis's house, Fiona

opened the car door. "Jane, please come inside. I hope
you don't mind my presumption, but I called Shelley
when I saw you sitting out here alone. Are you all
right?"

"Fine. I'm glad you called Shelley."

"What happened to the boy?"

"It wasn't Bobby. It was Phyllis. She's dead."

Fiona put her hand to her mouth. "Oh, no. Your
friend! Oh, Jane, I'm so sorry. How awful for you.
Come right inside."

Fiona got Jane comfortably settled in her kitchen with
a plaid wool blanket over her knees and a hot water
bottle under her feet. She seemed to be operating on
the premise that if she could get Jane warm, everything
else would be solved. In other circumstances, Jane
would have been amused by these terribly civilized an-
tics. As it was, she was feeling stupefied by recent
events. The heat was making her sleepy, too. If only
she could go back to bed and get a new start on this
day with no bad news.

Fiona had just handed her a cup of hot, strong, sweet
tea when Shelley rushed into the kitchen. "Fiona, your
maid let me in. Dear God, what's happened. Jane, are
you hurt?"

"No, it's Phyllis. She's dead."

"Oh, no!"

"Was it a heart attack?" Fiona asked, pouring another cup of tea for Shelley. "She looked quite healthy,
and she wasn't old. Only our age, wasn't she?"

"It wasn't a heart attack. It was murder."

"Murder!" Shelley and Fiona said in chorus.

"She was stabbed, I think. There was a terrible
amount of blood."

"You saw her?" Shelley asked. "Jane, how awful—
Fiona!"

Fiona had staggered against the kitchen counter and

was slowly crumpling. Jane and Shelley leaped forward together, caught her, and managed to get her into a chair. Forcing her head down between her knees, Shelley whispered, "I should have warned you. She's funny about blood. I saw her nick her finger once cutting a radish, and she keeled right over into the salad."

"I'm so sorry," Fiona said, sitting up straight. "How utterly stupid of me." The color was returning to her face, and she gave herself a little shake before standing up. "Jane, sit back down, and cover yourself with that blanket. You still look chilled."

Jane willingly did as she was told, not that she would mind falling into a restful little faint for a few minutes.

Shelley sat down across from her. "Jane, what do you know about this? Who would kill Phyllis, and why?"

"They don't know. I think it was a mistake. I mean, I think whoever did it meant to kill Bobby, not her." She explained about the rooms and about Bobby having the master suite.

"I don't know. That assumes the killer knew the layout of the house," Shelley said.

"Not necessarily," Fiona commented, now recovered. "You can tell from the outside that the bigger room must be the one that adjoins the deck. In fact, the way the staircase is set up, you'd assume the smaller room was just a closet or something unless you opened the door. I used to take food and magazines over occasionally to the old lady who lived there, and I was quite surprised to discover that it was a bedroom."

Shelley nodded. "All right. So somebody tried to kill him and got Phyllis by mistake. Who would that be? Aside from anybody unlucky enough to have met him. God! The police must have a world of suspects."

"There's another possibility," Jane said. "What if Bobby himself did it?"

"Is he really that awful?" Fiona asked with amazement. "She was his mother!"

"I've read that most murders are committed by family members," Jane said. "I think he could have done it. What I don't see is why he would. She was his meal ticket."

"But he didn't have the sense to treat her well," Shelley said. "If he'd had any brains at all, he'd have been buttering her up. He'd have been buttering *us* up, for that matter, to impress her."

"Meal ticket? What do you mean?" Fiona asked.

"That's right. You don't know the story of how she came by him, do you, Fiona?" Jane explained what she'd learned the day before about Bobby's origin.

"I had no idea," Fiona said, when Jane had completed the explanation. "Albert told me how she'd gone on and on about having found a long lost son when he took her over to see the house, but I assumed she was a widow. You mean there's a discontented husband somewhere? I should think he'd be the first one to consider."

"I imagine the police are considering him pretty strongly," Jane said. "But he's somewhere in the Caribbean, I assume."

"People can be hired for that sort of thing," Shelley put in.

"I know, but I'm sure that's not it. If Chet were driven to killing her, it would have to be a crime of passion. A sudden fit of rage. He loved her too much to get rid of her so coldly. Besides, there was no need. If he wanted her out of his life, all he had to do was divorce her."

"And pay a huge alimony," Shelley said.

"I don't think it would matter to him. He's got so much more money than he can ever spend, and I'm certain Phyllis wouldn't have asked for much. He would have known that about her. No, the one Chet might have wanted to get rid of was Bobby, not Phyllis. Bobby was really the one wrecking his happy life.''

The three women sat silently for a moment, contemplating. Finally Shelley said, ''Go back to this theory of yours about Bobby being the killer. Was he there?''

''Oh, yes. In all his radiant glory. Hung over and being thoroughly nasty.''

''He came in about one o'clock,'' Fiona added. ''At least somebody did. There was door slamming and swearing that woke me up. I assumed it was several people, but it could have been just one noisy one talking to himself.''

Shelley considered. ''I don't know, Jane. He's brash, but I don't think he's got that much nerve. To kill his mother, then stay in the house waiting to be found. Who called the police, by the way?''

''I didn't think to ask. I guess he did.''

''No, I don't think he'd have the balls for that. He's arrogant, but I suspect he's a coward at heart. Most arrogant people are. Besides, how *would* he benefit from her death? He'd have to know that Chet would cut off the funds to him the minute Phyllis was gone.''

''But who knows?'' Jane insisted. ''Suppose Chet had turned a lot of assets over to Phyllis and she'd willed them to Bobby? Chet's a lot older than Phyllis and might have thought it would be easier for her to get along someday without him if half their assets were in her name.''

Fiona said, ''That could be. A lot of couples prefer dividing assets to having them in joint custody. It doesn't make sense legally, but some people still do it. If that were true, the boy could have it all at once rather than at the pleasure of his mother.''

''I can't imagine Phyllis having the sense to make a will,'' Jane said. ''But maybe, under the circumstances, she did. But would Bobby know what was in it?''

Shelley gave her a pitying look. "Phyllis? She told him everything. You saw them together. She was desperate to find anything to arouse his interest in her. And I'm sure talk about a will would do it.''

"I think you may be right. Now, while we're considering domestic suspects, what about John Wagner?''

"John Wagner!'' Fiona exclaimed. "You don't mean the John Wagner who lives over on Oak Lane, do you?''

Jane nodded.

"He's a perfectly odious man. I wouldn't put anything past him.'' Noticing her companions' startled expressions, she explained, "Shortly after we moved here, he approached Albert about a community fund-raising project to buy a couple of lots and turn them into a park. Albert was disposed to be helpful until your Mr. Wagner laid out the plans. The way he saw it, I would contribute virtually all the money, Albert would do all the work, and Wagner would get all the credit, including having the park named for him. Of course, Albert refused, and Wagner became extremely offensive about our finances and status.''

Jane could well imagine. He probably made some crack about it really being Richie Divine's money, not theirs. At least, that was the sort of thing he'd say.

Fiona's face was flushed. The memory really rankled. "I'm sorry. That's entirely beside the point. I shouldn't have mentioned it.''

"No, I'm glad you did,'' Jane assured her. "Let me tell you the things he said about me when we were on the volleyball team—''

"Jane, that's hardly relevant,'' Shelley said. "We're agreed that he's a son of a bitch. But does that mean he'd murder his stepmother? And if so, why wait all these years?''

"Well, for one thing, she was in Chicago, right under his nose. I don't think she'd been back here since he became an adult. It would have been a lot harder to fly into the island and get out again without being noticed. But that doesn't matter. I don't think he would have killed her. I think he would have killed Bobby, or tried to. See, it's the same with Chet or John Wagner. The thing that changed in their lives was the addition of Bobby. It was when he came along that everything started to go wrong."

"How would he have known where they were?" Fiona asked. "She only saw the house yesterday afternoon and moved right in."

"But she called him from my house and invited him over."

"To your house?" Shelley exclaimed. "Would he dare?"

"Sure. He had no idea he offended me. But he didn't come anyway. He did go see her, but at the house next door later last night. So he knew the house—"

Shelley caught her train of thought. "She probably showed him around, and he would have known which room she was in."

"Maybe not."

"Look, Jane, half the time you're arguing that Bobby was the intended victim and half the time that he was the murderer. You can't have it both ways."

"But I want it to be one or the other," Jane admitted. "We don't know enough to guess what happened, but I'm positive Bobby had something to do with it. He's far too horrible to simply be an innocent bystander."

Fiona's maid came into the kitchen looking rattled. "Excuse me, Mrs. Howard, but there's a man to see you. A policeman."

"Thank you, Celia. Don't be alarmed. He's just

making inquiries about what happened next door last
night. He may want to talk to you, too."

"I'm going home," Jane said. "He'll have a fit if he
finds me here. Thanks for the tea, Fiona."

She and Shelley slipped out the back door. "Is that
your Detective VanDyne calling on Fiona?" Shelley
asked as they walked away.

"*My* VanDyne?" Jane scoffed. But she did like the
sound of that phrase.

For once, Jane was happy to come home to a messy house; it gave her something to do. She fed the pets, then cleaned up the rubble the kids always left in their mad dash to school. The milk lake was the worst part. Willard had run through it and left sticky tracks all over the kitchen. She mopped it up and ran down to the basement to wash the towel she'd thrown in to soak up the worst. It was one of her best towels, and she noted with irritation that it was beginning to fray along one edge.

Funny how linens and light bulbs all seemed to give up at the same time, no matter when they were purchased. She'd have to buy some more towels—a thought which led her to consider her financial status. These plush beauties had been purchased when Steve was alive and bringing home money weekly. Now she got a check once a month from her mother-in-law which represented Steve's share of the Jeffry family pharmacies' profits. There was also the interest on the CDs that she had put Steve's life insurance money into. But she had always put that back into the kids' college accounts. Sometime soon she would have to give some serious thought to getting a job.

An old aunt of hers had given her advice the day after Steve's death which she had followed just because Aunt May was so forceful and certain of herself. Aunt May had said the one thing a new widow must do is absolutely nothing. Make no changes, no unnecessary decisions for a full year. It had been good advice, keeping Jane from acting on all the crazy notions that had occurred to her in those first weeks, but soon the year of grace would be over.

Would Chet Wagner make impulsive changes and decisions? she wondered as she closed the lid of the washing machine. Was "do nothing" the sort of advice a successful businessman could or should follow? Of course, most men don't have the things that keep their feet on the ground like most women do when death leaves holes in the middle of their lives. A woman still had wash to do, meals to cook, pets and children to look after. Grief simply couldn't go full throttle when you're cleaning burnt oatmeal off the bottom of a pan. Most women had friends to rally around, too. She'd seen a television play once in which an old lady said of a girl in trouble, "She probably went home to her mother. Women turn to women in time of trouble."

Poor Chet. Men didn't seem to turn to other men very often in time of trouble. Did he have a friend to turn to? He certainly couldn't count on his son John for sympathy and support. John Wagner wasn't the nurturing sort. Jane had never met the other son; perhaps he was a nicer person. Of course, Chet had tons of people who worked for him. Those who were bright and ambitious would at least pretend sympathy and look for opportunities to help him. Maybe that would be enough.

Jane came back upstairs and went to work on tidying up the living room, getting ready for more Christmas decorations. She picked up things the kids had left and took them up to dump in their rooms. She plumped cushions, halfheartedly ran a dust cloth over the major flat surfaces, and hauled the recalcitrant vacuum cleaner out of the front hall closet. But on her first swoop with it, she sucked up a penny that crashed around hideously for a second before the machine moaned to a smelly stop. "Damn!" she exclaimed, unplugging the monster and flipping it over onto its back to operate.

As she knelt, she caught a glimpse of white under the nearest chair. It was one of Phyllis's knitting bags. Jane crawled over, pulled it out, and peered in the top. It was Bobby's crimson sweater. Never to be completed. Jane pulled out a sleeve and looked at the elaborate cable pattern, done apparently on size two or three needles. She could feel the sharp-cornered edge of a knitting book in the bag. Maybe she could finish the sweater for Phyllis. It seemed a fitting tribute, especially given how difficult it would be for an amateur like Jane. But what would she do with it, if and when she ever finished? Give it to Bobby, as Phyllis had intended? God, no! The day would never dawn that Jane would so much as slip a stitch for Bobby Bryant.

She shoved the sweater sleeve back into the plastic bag, wondering what to do with it, when there was a knock on the door. Willard, naturally, went quite mad. As he went flying by, barking like there was a mob of cossacks about to break down the doors, Jane reached out and grabbed his collar and nearly jerked both of them right off their feet. Shoving him down the basement steps, she went to the front door and discovered Mel VanDyne. Of course! He *would* visit when there was a dead vacuum cleaner with its guts spilling out in the middle of the living room.

"Come in. Let's sit in the kitchen," she said. "Have you learned anything yet?"

"Nothing worthwhile. I've been interviewing neighbors. I hope you'll tell me what they wouldn't themselves."

"You think a neighbor killed her?"

"No, I don't. According to you and Mrs. Howard,

Mrs. Wagner just flitted in and bought the house yesterday. Nobody'd ever heard of her or met her before. It seems unlikely that anybody could develop a murderous hatred of her in such a short time. Still, I need to check it out."

Jane had poured them coffee and sat down across the table from him. At least she'd cleaned up the milk lake and cleared the crumbs. He wouldn't go away with greasy elbows from sitting at her table. If he wasn't impressed by her neatness, at least he wouldn't be having a little chat with the Board of Health about her. "I get it. This is a perfectly pointless line of inquiry, so it's okay to talk to me about it."

He grinned over the top of his coffee cup. *Oh, those teeth!* "Tell me about the Howards and Mr. Finch anyway."

"Tell me what you think of them first."

"All right. Mrs. Howard is a nice Englishwoman, and Mr. Finch is a not very nice American. There's also a house behind on the next street, but the people are out of town."

"The neighbors think Mr. Finch poisons dogs and cats that come in his yard."

"I know. The local police have a fat file of complaints but no proof. Mrs. Wagner didn't know him, did she?"

"Of course not. How would she? She only lived in the house for a few hours. When *did* Phyllis die?"

"Don't know yet. The coroner's first guess was between midnight and four. Her son says she spoke to him when he came in, but he has no idea when that was. Thinks it was around one. That's when Mrs. Howard says she heard a voice or voices. Do you know this Finch character?"

"No. We've got a nodding acquaintance, as my mother would say. I see him working on his lawn, which is sacrosanct. And I pass him in the aisles of the grocery store. My kids are afraid of him, but that's probably because he's the neighborhood ogre. He's yelled at them a time or two for cutting across the corner of the yard. In fact, he called me once when Mike was little to tell me what a bad mannered child he was. I never knew quite what it was about.''

"You think he's a killer type?"

"Of dogs and cats, yes. But unless Phyllis ran across his precious lawn with a Rototiller, I can't imagine why he'd have the least interest in her, let alone a desire to kill her.''

"Fair enough. When I went over to talk to him, he tried to make me take off my shoes before I could come into the house. My impression is that murder is altogether too messy an activity for him. What about Mrs. Howard?''

"Fiona? You know who she is, don't you? She's Richie Divine's widow.''

VanDyne set his coffee cup down with a clatter. "You're kidding! *The* Richie Divine? Of course—Fiona Divine. I should have recognized the name Fiona.''

"I think she'd be pleased that you didn't.''

"I had a lot of interest in his death. My sister was visiting friends in Seattle and went to his last concert. She was at some sort of slumber party when she heard the radio bulletin that his plane had crashed in the Pacific on the way to his next concert. Called home in the middle of the night and woke the whole family up to tell us. I always thought there was something suspicious about it, even then.''

"Why? Tragic, yes. But suspicious?''

"Don't you remember? He'd gotten into some kind of flap with organized crime—they were skimming profits from his tours. He actually testified against his own business manager, who then ratted on everybody he knew.''

"I had forgotten that. You mean the mob had something to do with his plane going down?''

"There wasn't any proof that I know of. But the plane didn't just run out of gas and fall into the ocean. It blew up in midair first. They never found enough bits of the plane—or the passengers—to reconstruct what happened.''

"Oh, ugh. I was happier not knowing that.''

"Sorry.''

"Did you ever stop to think how many entertainers have died in plane crashes? Will Rogers, Glenn Miller—''

"Buddy Holly, the Big Bopper, and Richie Valens in the same one,'' Mel added.

"Rick Nelson, Patsy Cline—''

"Interesting, but beside the point, if you don't mind my mentioning it. Did Mrs. Wagner know Fiona?''

"No, not before I took her over with me to move some boxes of stuff for the bazaar. Phyllis did mention knowing somebody who knew Fiona, but she couldn't remember who it was. To be honest, I think Phyllis was fudging the truth there. I think she'd just read about Fiona in fan magazines.''

"So they'd never met?''

"No, I'm sure they hadn't. Women who have met before always at least pretend to remember each other. Neither of them did that.''

"Okay. Who else did Mrs. Wagner know in Chicago?''

"Nobody that I know of. I believe the aunt she lived with in the old days died some years ago. She might know Bobby's adopted family. She told me some story about the stepmother not getting along with him, but that could just be Bobby's version. I don't know that she ever met them. Chet was apparently the one who traced him down, as a surprise to her.''

"God, what a surprise. More of a shock, I'd think."

"She adored him."

VanDyne stared at her.

"Incredible, but true," Jane insisted.

"Did she say anything at all that might lead you to think his adopted family had anything against her?''

"No, in fact, reading between the lines, I got the impression that they were thrilled to have him out of their hair. Of course, that could just be my interpretation of how I'd feel. Have you talked to them yet?''

"No, the father and stepmother are out of town. A vacation to Florida. Of course, with air travel being so fast and easy—" Suddenly he seemed to catch himself in the midst of gossiping with a civilian. "Thanks for your help," he said, starting to get up.

"Wait a minute!" Jane ordered. "You've asked me for a lot of information you didn't much want anyway, and you haven't told me anything. I've got some questions of my own. For a start, who called you in?''

"Bobby himself. Says he got up to go to the bathroom, glanced in her room, and saw she was dead. By the time the officers got there, he'd passed out.''

"Do you think he'd do that if he was the one who killed her?''

"Who can tell? He might have been so drunk he wasn't making sense. Or he could have been so stewed that he'd forgotten that he'd killed her. Or he might have figured out that nobody else was likely to discover her for a good long time, and he'd better brazen it out.''

"Maybe. Have you located Chet yet?''

"No, he's not on that island they own, and nobody seems to know where he's gone. His assistant has promised to let me know the second he's found.''

"You aren't still suspecting him, are you?''

"I'd be both crazy and negligent not to. How well do you know this guy?"

"I hardly knew him at all, but I know he adored Phyllis."

"Still? Or seventeen years ago?"

"What do you mean?"

"You got the idea that he adored her from *her*, didn't you?" VanDyne said. "Look, if she'd come here without that obnoxious son and just talked about him, wouldn't you have formed a different sort of impression? That he was a terrific kid who loved her? Maybe it's the same with her husband."

"I'm not convinced. But maybe you're right. So you think Chet killed her?"

He set his coffee cup by the sink and started strolling toward the front door. "You know I'm not supposed to discuss my opinions with the general public."

"That just means you don't have any idea yet—and I'm not the 'general public.' I'm Phyllis's friend. Probably the last person to see her alive except for the killer."

VanDyne had reached the front door and was resting his hand lightly on the handle, giving her a long, cool look. "Yes, that's quite true, isn't it."

Jane felt her heart sink "Why—why you *jerk*! You didn't come here for a friendly chat. You came here to interrogate me. Am I one of your suspects?"

"At this stage, everybody is," he said calmly. There was something that looked suspiciously like a smile starting at the corners of his mouth.

"Not me! Get out!"

"Okay," he said, cheerfully ignoring her fury. "I'll see you later—Jane."

She slammed the door behind him, then leaned on it, listening to Willard's renewed frenzy of barking. She wasn't sure whether she wanted to laugh or cry. He was really maddening. But maddening was a lot better than boring.

Jane found herself wondering what it would be like to talk with him about something other than crime. What if he did actually ask her out sometime? What would they discuss? Where would they go? Just how much would they find they had in common? Would he find her the slightest bit interesting if he weren't trying to get specific information from her? And would she find him interesting once she got her fill of admiring his smile? She'd reached the dizzy point of speculating on what it would be like to kiss him when Willard, still incarcerated in the basement, let out a pitiful howl.

"I know just how you feel," she said to him.

——14——

Jane released Willard and went back to work on the vacuum cleaner. But she'd hardly gotten it together before there was another knock on the door. She opened it to find her friend Suzie Williams from down the street. "Jesus H. God, Jane, can't you shut that dog up?" Suzie asked.

She was a big, gorgeous woman who made a mockery of the entire theory of dieting. Built roughly along the lines of Mae West, she had masses of naturally curly, naturally platinum blond hair—or at least, it was artfully contrived to look natural. A buyer and saleswoman for the foundations section of the local department store, Suzie was also the living denial of the career woman. Though she was extremely successful at her job, she made no bones about her constant search for a man to first inhabit her bed and then, if sexually satisfactory, to fill her checkbook with lovely money that *he* made. In addition, she was the most refreshingly vulgar person Jane had ever known.

"Come in, Suzie. What are you doing at large in the middle of the day?"

"Watch that 'at large' talk," Suzie said, sailing through to the kitchen. "I was on my way home for lunch and saw a red MG in your driveway. So I cruised the block until it left. That was our old pal Detective VanDyne, wasn't it?"

"Yes, it was. I swear, that man makes me crazy."

"That good, huh?"

"That's *not* what I mean—more's the pity."

"Cut through the crap, Jane. What was he doing here? If you're screwing him, I want every juicy detail. Then I want to know how I can get in line to be next. From the looks of his car and clothes, he makes a decent living." She fished in her purse, brought out a couple of candy canes, and offered one to Jane.

"No, thanks. I'm not screwing Mel VanDyne. Only daydreaming."

"Oh, it's 'Mel' now, is it? Jane, I'm short on time, and I'm missing my lunch to butt in here. Aren't you going to offer me a sandwich while you tell me everything?"

"I haven't got any bread that doesn't have green fuzz on it. Let's go get a hamburger instead."

They got into Suzie's car and went to the local McDonald's. While hunched hungrily over Big Macs ("None of that salad crap for me. I have to keep up my strength to spend an afternoon fitting corsets," Suzie said), Jane explained why Mel VanDyne had been at her house.

Suzie daintily chewed the last of her second order of large fries and said, "I'd opt for that asshole Finch. I'd like to see him in the clink whether he did it or not."

"What have you got against Mr. Finch?"

"Not half as much as he tried to put against me. I was out for a walk one day last summer, and as I passed his house, he latches on to me and starts yammering about his new toolshed. I guess it was the silly bastard's idea of flirting. Well, I didn't have much of anything I was in a hurry to do, and I figured, hell, why not let the old fool have the thrill of showing the damned thing to me? Well! He lures me into the shed thing, which reeks of insecticide, and all of a sudden he's all hands and pelvis.''

"What did you do?"

"Kneed him in the crotch, of course. That really jarred his dentures. Silly old fool.''

"He's not so old, is he?"

"I guess not. Only fifty or so, but that old-maid prissy sort of man always seems older. I'd chalked him up as gay before, which is why the whole thing took me so off guard. Men don't often take me by surprise.''

"Suzie, I think you ought to tell VanDyne about this. Finch might have tried to rape Phyllis and ended up killing her.''

"Rape? He wouldn't do that."

"But you said you had to fight him off."

"Oh, it wasn't so much that I *had* to as I *got* to. I was never in any danger. I was just pissed at him. No, I don't think Finch is really a strong possibility, much as I'd like him to be, and much as I'd like an excuse to have a chummy little visit with Vandyne. I think it's the husband or the stepson. Murder usually runs in families, you know.''

"But her husband loved her."

"Horseshit! You weigh love against paying alimony, and love loses every time. Even my husband—asshole that he is—was real generous about everything until we got divorced. But it's like pulling teeth to get my child support every month—and he's crazy about our kid; he just can't stand the idea of me so much as getting to look at his money as it goes by.''

"But Chet has lots of money. More than he needs."

"Come on, Jane! Nobody thinks they have more than they need. All the greed or drive or whatever the hell it takes to get it and keep it can't ever be turned off.''

"Maybe you're right."

"You can bet on it. I've got to get back to work.

There's a world of women out there who are too old to jiggle and crying out for my attention. You through with your lunch?''

As Suzie dropped her off at home, she said, "Oh, Jane, I nearly forgot. I got Monday off work to help with the bazaar. And I've always got Friday afternoons, so I can help you tomorrow, if you need me."

"We sure do. I'd nearly forgotten about the bazaar with all this other business."

Jane spent the remainder of the afternoon doing one of her assigned jobs for the church bazaar. Seated at the kitchen table with the phone and her list of potential helpers, she managed to get a patchy sort of schedule worked out. She, Shelley, and Fiona were doing all the sorting and setting up and would also work the actual sale. But many more people were needed before and after.

Examples of the best of the merchandise would be displayed in the foyer at church the coming Sunday morning—though there was a bit of grumbling from the pious about this blatant display of commercialism. One woman carried on as if they were planning to be hawking plastic Santas right from the altar. To these folks, Jane gave her standard speech about the church not being able to function in a real world on faith alone. She had this prim little speech down by rote, and it quelled most of them into agreeing to help in some capacity.

The selected items would remain there to be shown again at the church choir concert that night. With some difficulty, Jane managed to find volunteers to gather up the display examples after the concert and take them back to Fiona's.

Monday morning, the sale would begin, and Jane needed a whole new set of people to work that day. Some volunteers would blanket the neighborhood with signs, and others would work at the actual sale. It wasn't hard to find people for this job, which was considered the fun part. It was also a way to be visibly charitable. Women who hadn't lifted a finger or checkbook to help in any other capacity volunteered for an hour or two of sale work with the air of a queen offering to confer her presence on the masses.

The hardest part was finding people to help clear out what was left. The previous bazaar chairman had warned them that the number of leftovers could be overwhelming, and it was imperative to have people who had not contributed items be responsible for what got thrown out and what got saved for future sales. The year before last, she confided, the Parslow sisters took on the job, and ninety percent of what was left had been created lovingly—if tackily—by them. There had been tears and hysteria.

Each call required a certain amount of pleasant chat. Unlike dealing with paid employees, Jane couldn't just briskly tell people what they were supposed to do and hang up. She had to listen politely to elaborate excuses that had to do with children, husbands, chicken pox, school programs, hysterectomies, and out of town family visits. Some were willing enough to volunteer but wanted to extract some promise or another from Jane in return. By the time she was done, she'd agreed to run for secretary of the local M.A.D.D. group, drive a load of kindergartners to see a greenhouse in February as part of their Growing Things unit, operate the cotton candy machine at the P.T.A. carnival in April, and chaperone the midterm high school band booster pizza party in January.

And while she talked, Jane crocheted madly, silently mouthing "Triple, triple, triple, single—" all the while. Just before she had to pause in her scheduling efforts and start her car pool runs, Jane laid out the afghan on the living room floor. It was really getting to be very pretty, and if she didn't eat or sleep between now and Sunday, there was a chance she could finish it.

She'd half formed the thought that maybe Phyllis could help her with it before she remembered that Phyllis was dead. Her busy afternoon had almost made her forget. She suddenly felt a great sense of loss for a woman she'd never really known very well. Phyllis Wagner would never help with an afghan, or finish a sweater for her son, or do anything. Jane had tears in her eyes as she shoved Willard off the afghan and gathered it up to work on while she waited for the kids.

Jane had worried about telling the children, especially Todd, about Phyllis's death. But because she fudged on the truth (leading them to believe the death was natural) and because they'd never heard Jane talk about her friend Phyllis, much less met her, they took the news well, if not to say downright callously. "That's too bad, Mom. When are we having dinner? I've got to go to brass section practice at seven," Mike said when he got home.

"I bet you feel sad," Todd said, then turned his attention back to teasing Willard with a potato chip.

Katie, surprisingly, showed the most sympathy, even if it was badly expressed. "That's awful, Mom. I guess someday I'll get old and my friends will start dying, too."

"I'm not old!"

"You know what I mean."

"I'm not sure I do."

"Mom, you know that yellow Esprit sweater at the mall? The one I made you come see? Jenny says she was there last night, and it was on sale."

A full price version and the coordinated slacks were already wrapped in Christmas paper in Jane's bedroom closet. "I'm sorry, Katie, I told you no more yellow sweaters. You already have two."

"Yeah, but you borrowed one and got mustard on it, remember?"

"Mom, somebody at the door for you. A man," Mike said as he passed through on the way to the refrigerator.

Wondering how long it might have taken Mike to deliver this news if he hadn't been hungry, Jane tucked in her blouse and said, "Katie, put that dog in the basement before he notices a stranger in the house."

She half expected (hoped?) the caller was Mel VanDyne. She was surprised to see a man she didn't recognize for a second, then she realized this was the Scourge of the Volleyball Court. "You don't know me, Mrs. Jeffry, but I'm John Wagner."

"Please come in." Leading the way, she took him to the living room. Todd had the television on, looking for something to watch. "Scoot, kiddo," she said. He tossed her the controller, an object she'd never understood. Rather than show her ignorance, she set the gadget on an end table without trying to turn off the set. "We have met," she told her guest. "At volleyball a year or so ago."

His look of surprise turned to embarrassment. "Oh, yes. I do remember. I had to quit playing. My wife threatened to leave me. I turn into a sort of Hitler when I play games."

Jane's previous opinion of him crumbled. Could this self-effacing man be the same monster who'd called her a pinhead three times in one game? "It's a good thing she stopped you. You know what happened to Hitler. Mr. Wagner, I'm sorry about your stepmother."

"I came to offer my sympathy to you as well. It must be a terrible blow, as close as you were to her. I remember her mentioning you. She was always quoting from your letters.''

Jane felt as if she'd been stabbed—right to the heart. ''I enjoyed her letters, too,'' she mumbled, agonizingly aware that she couldn't recall so much as a single phrase from those boring epistles.

They were both silent for a moment, then both started to speak at once. ''Company first,'' Jane said with a smile.

''I came to ask a favor of you. The police have asked me to come over and look at her things. To see if there's anything among them that isn't hers—in case the killer dropped something. Of course, my father would know best, if anybody could locate him, but I'd sort of like to spare him the job, if I could. Besides, it just seems a job a woman ought to do for another woman. I wondered if you'd be willing to help me.''

''I'd be happy to, but I won't have any more idea than you do what belongs to her and what doesn't.''

''Oh, but you knew her so well. I'm sure you can tell just by looking if it's something she'd have or not.''

Worse and worse! There wasn't a Jewish mother who ever lived who could match this man for laying on guilt.

''I'll do what I can, of course. Do you mean no one has told your father yet?''

''Nobody can find him. He's just not used to accounting for his movements to anybody but Phy—Oh, my God—!''

He was staring past Jane as if he'd seen a ghost. Turning her head, Jane saw it, too—a portrait photo of Phyllis Wagner was on the television screen. She quickly picked up the mysterious controller, fidgeted frantically for a few seconds before finding the volume control.

''. . . wife of entrepreneur Chester Wagner. The former Chicagoan reportedly died of stab wounds. Police located her husband this afternoon at a downtown hotel under an assumed name. . . . ''

On the screen a fit, tanned, silver-haired man was being escorted to a police car. At least he wasn't handcuffed, and without the narration, he would have looked like a diplomat with his own security men. ''Oh, shit—'' John Wagner whispered, leaning forward.

The next shot was of Mel VanDyne shaking his head and holding a palm out toward the camera.

''No, we are merely questioning Mr. Wagner in regard to his wife's death. There has been no arrest. You will be informed when there is.''

The station cut to a commercial, and Jane and Wagner were left staring at each other wordlessly.

15

"I'm not going to let this happen. Those bastards aren't going to pin this on my father," John Wagner exclaimed, standing suddenly and striding toward the door. "Excuse me, Mrs. Jeffry." With that, he was gone.

Jane sat quietly for a minute after the door slammed, then picked up the controller and started cruising through channels. It was time for the local news, and each of the major stations had something to say about Phyllis's death. All the reports focused on Chet, as if Phyllis herself were nothing more than an important object belonging to him. Of course, what was there to say about her except that she was Chet's wife? That she once made lonely old people happy with tatted ornaments? That she was a superb knitter? That she loved a long lost son who didn't deserve her? Hardly.

One station showed a picture of the house with the yellow plastic police barricades. Another had dredged up a file photo of Phyllis in a crowd of second string international celebrities. A third went on at quite some length about Chet's financial empire and showed a shot of the island house—or was it the hotel? Jane couldn't tell.

She learned nothing more than she'd heard earlier about the case, but she did see a familiar face on one report. It was the same scene she'd seen on the other

117

channel, Chet being led to a car by two plainclothes officers, but it was shot from a slightly different angle, and in the background two men were conversing over an open notebook. One of them was a big, late-middle-aged man in a somewhat wrinkled gray suit and a fedora hat right out of the forties.

He was Jane's Uncle Jim—not a real uncle but an honorary one, her father's lifelong best friend. Formerly of the army, for many years with the Chicago police department, he remained close to Jane, especially since Steve died and left her "a helpless widow" in his words. She turned off the television, went to the kitchen, and dialed his precinct telephone number. He'd gone for the day, she was told. There was no answer at his apartment yet.

While she waited, she got out some ground beef and onions to brown. Ten minutes later, when they were nearly done, Shelley came over. "Jane, did you see the news? Your friend was all over it."

"I know. Did you see my Uncle Jim in the background? I'm waiting for him to get home so I can pump him for information."

"He's not crazy about giving you inside information, is he?"

"I just want 'outside' information," Jane said, carefully draining the meat and onion mixture and adding beans and tomato sauce. "John Wagner was here. Shelley, it was weird. He was nice. Nice!"

"Jane, have you considered getting psychiatric help? You're going to clog up your disposal if you don't run cold water."

Jane turned on the water. "I mean it about John Wagner. He even apologized for being so hateful about volleyball."

"He must have really wanted something."

"From me?" Jane asked, shaking chili seasoning

into the pot and stirring. "All he asked was that I help him look over Phyllis's things to see if anything was there that shouldn't be. Of course, he'd barely gotten here when the news came on, and he dashed off. I've never seen a man look so upset. He even seemed genuinely sorry about Phyllis, and then there was that picture of Chet being led away, and John turned the color of cauliflower."

"I've got to go back to fixing dinner," Shelley said. "Call and tell me what you find out from your Uncle Jim, will you?"

"Say, Shelley—what are you doing after dinner?"

"Nothing planned. Why?"

"Well, I'd like to do what John Wagner was asking— look through Phyllis's things—and get it over with. He made me feel horribly guilty, saying I'd know what was hers just because I knew her so well. The fact is, you and I might know if something isn't hers just because we're women. I mean, Steve once saw me using a nail whitening pencil and said he'd always wondered what they were. His mother always had one around. He thought it was some secret feminine hygiene thing you don't talk about. I guess that's sort of an opposite example of what I mean, but—"

"I get it anyhow. I don't think you'll find anything interesting, but sure—I'll come along. How do you plan to get into the house?"

"Last I heard, Bobby was staying there."

Shelley shuddered. "I forgot about him. Do you think we ought to get near him? What if he is the murderer?"

"There's safety in numbers. Besides, he'd have no reason to do anything to us."

Jane fed everybody, drove Mike to band practice, dropped Todd at a friend's house, and took Katie to her pal Jenny's, whose mother had offered to take them to a teen fashion show at the mall. Certain they all had rides home, Jane came back for Shelley. "Let me give Uncle Jim one more try," she said, stamping the snow off her boots at Shelley's kitchen door.

This time she got him.

"Hey, Janey. You calling to uninvite me to Saturday dinner?" he asked.

"Don't get your hopes up. Mike is counting on you coming to his concert, and I've already got the sauerbraten marinating. I'm calling because I saw you on television this afternoon."

"Oh, yeah. The Wagner thing. VanDyne is in charge. Did you know that?"

"I not only know it, I'm a suspect. Phyllis was a friend of mine. In fact, she'd come to Chicago to visit me."

"My God, Jane! The things you get into."

"I didn't get into it. It came looking for me. Uncle Jim, what do you know about this?"

"Up until now, nothing. I was just asked to have a man or two at the exits in case there was trouble. There wasn't. Jane, if I'd known you were involved—"

"Don't get upset. I'm not involved. But I want to know what's happening. Have they actually arrested Chet Wagner?"

"Not that I know of. Like I say, I didn't take much interest. I had the idea it was just a matter of time. Give me an hour or two to see what I can find out. I'll call you back. You home?"

Jane paused. "Ah—no. I'm at Shelley's, and we're going—going Christmas shopping."

But the pause had alerted him. "Jane," he said menacingly. "You stay away from all this, understand?"

"Well, of course. Don't be ridiculous. I'll call you back when I get home." She hung up the phone and said, "Let's get out of here quick before he decides to come babysit me."

The police boundary tape was gone, and the rented Jaguar was in the driveway. Bobby came to the door with a drink in his hand. "Yeah? Whaddaya want?"

"I'm Jane Jeffry, and this is Shelley Nowack. Remember us from yesterday? I loaned your mother a book, and I wondered if it would be all right if I went up and got it back." Jane was rather proud of this little story. It had crossed her mind on the way over that asking to browse through Phyllis's belongings for clues might not please Bobby. And if he was the killer, they certainly didn't want to offer him a motive to harm them.

"Yeah, I guess it's okay. The cops have already gone through all her stuff," he said, apparently not fooled in the least by Jane's story.

He opened the door and allowed them in. Jane noted that he was already making a shambles of the house. Clothing was strewn around, beer bottles were making rings on the dining room table, and several ashtrays overflowed with butts.

Bobby slouched toward the kitchen, leaving Shelley and Jane to their own devices. That was good; he didn't intend to stand over them while they went through her things.

At the top of the stairs, Shelley grabbed Jane's arm. "Look at that!" she said, pointing toward the master suite. In addition to the unmade bed, clothing and suitcases flung everywhere, there was an elaborate sound system on the far wall next to the door to the deck.

"That wasn't here this morning," Jane whispered.

"I've been pricing this stuff for Paul for Christmas, and take my word for it, that's at least $3000 worth of equipment."

"I guess he ran out and used his mother's credit cards to the limit before Chet thought to have them shut off. What a bastard!"

Turning their backs on the evidence of Bobby's greed, they went into the small bedroom Phyllis had died in. Jane let out a long breath of relief. The blood-soaked mattress and bedding had been removed. The rest of the room, however, was in chaos. Suitcases gaped open with clothing tumbling out. The perfume and makeup on the dressing table looked like someone had rummaged through it with a heavy hand. "The police went through this. They certainly made a mess," Jane said, frowning.

"I don't think this is the way the police would work. This has a distinctly Bobby look. I bet he was searching for something."

"But what?"

"Maybe he thought she had a lot of cash hidden in her suitcases. Maybe she did. That might account for the stereo and tape deck and all."

Jane looked around the room sadly. "This isn't right. We can't leave it this way. I wouldn't like Chet to ever see her things this way."

"Chet? Chet's probably in the slammer right now for having killed her."

"I know that, but I still don't believe he could have. Let's clean this up and get out."

The box springs were still on the bed frame, and the two women set the four big suitcases and the overnight case there to start filling them. Item by item they started picking up clothing, folding and repacking it. Everything was of excellent quality. Handmade French silk underwear, Scottish woolen skirts and dresses, a Bob Mackie evening dress, a stunning Michaele Vollbracht swimsuit, though God knew where she'd intended to wear that!

"Look at this," Shelley said. She'd picked up a magenta silk dressing gown with a pink appliquéd chrysanthemum. Underneath it on the floor was a needlepointed bag about the same dimensions as a briefcase. On the front, in satin stitch, were the initials P.F.W. "I bet he didn't even see this. If I were carrying important papers or extra emergency money, this is where I'd keep them. I wonder if the police noticed it."

Jane took the largest suitcase off the bed, and they sat down. Shelley slid the contents of the case out. The largest item was, of all things, a well-thumbed high school yearbook—an old one from a school in Pennsylvania. "Imagine your yearbook being so important you'd carry it around," Shelley said sadly. "I don't even know where mine is, and I don't care."

"I don't have one," Jane said. "I graduated from a school in Washington, D.C. that I'd only attended for the last semester. I think that was between Egypt and Germany."

"Look at this," Shelley said, flipping through the pages. "She not only carried it around, it's nearly worn out. She must have actually looked at the thing often. Why does that break my heart?"

"Because it's so typically Phyllis. What's in the envelopes?"

The first and thinnest of the two manila envelopes contained various documents; some papers having to do with Bobby's adoption and a number of pictures of him. Bobby sunbathing, Bobby diving, Bobby lounging on a deck chair, Bobby leaning on a balcony rail. In every one of them he had an arrogant smirk, as if thinking, Look where I am, world!

There were also some insurance papers, Phyllis's passport, her birth certificate, Bobby's passport, and a few faded old photos of a middle-aged woman with hat, hair, and clothes that looked like the picture was taken in the middle sixties. She looked like the kind of woman who really belonged on a farm, making pies. "I bet that's her aunt, the one who took her in. She died a few years ago. See, here's a clipping of the obituary notice," Jane said.

There were a lot of pictures of Chet, too, and Jane realized with a shock that he was really quite dynamic and youthful looking. Nothing like the grim, unremarkable man on the evening news. There were candid shots of the two of them dancing, sailing, swimming, playing shuffleboard on a cruise ship. One was a studio portrait of the two of them in silhouette, looking into each other's eyes. Sort of overdramatic and silly but touching just the same, because the look of love they were exchanging was obviously so genuine.

"I'm sorry we looked in this," Jane said. "It's like peeping into someone's bedroom window." She stacked the contents and slipped them back into the envelope.

The second envelope, the one that bulged, was full of knitting patterns, some clipped magazine articles about various crafts, and a plastic palletlike holder strung with samples of several dozen colors of yarn. Folded into a thick bundle were numerous letters and order forms for fabrics and fibers from places all over the world. There was also a long, flat, embossed leather case that opened to reveal a complete set of knitting needles in every size.

"Wicked looking things, aren't they?" Shelley said, gathering everything up to put back in the bag.

"If I were carrying around money, I'd have put it with the other legal documents in that first envelope, wouldn't you?" Jane said.

"Probably," Shelley said. As she rose to put the displaced suitcase back on the bed, she stopped and peered out the front window. "Somebody's stopped in front of the house."

"Damn! With my luck, it's either Mel Vandyne or my Uncle Jim. Either one of them will have a fit if they find me here snooping around."

"I think it's too late to escape. Two men are coming to the front door."

Jane stood up. "Might as well go down there and get chewed out and have it over with. Someday I'm going to write the definitive work on how to be in the wrong place at the wrong time."

16

Jane hesitated on the stairs, realizing it wasn't her house or her place to go to the door. But after a moment, when there was neither sound nor sight of Bobby, Shelley gave her a little shove, and they went down together The door opened, however, before they reached it. Chet and John Wagner came in, John pocketing a key. Chet looked like a strong man who'd lost a war. So must General Lee have appeared—grim, gray, and rigid, held together by dignity alone. John Wagner was keeping close to him, one hand hovering, ready to take his elbow to steady his father as if he were a fragile old man. John had the air of a man thrust uncomprehendingly into a nurturing role and extremely uncomfortable with it.

Jane stepped forward with her hand outstretched. "Chet, you probably don't remember me from the old days; I'm Jane Jeffry."

He took her hand in a firm grip and held it between both of his square, well-manicured hands. "Of course I remember. You haven't changed at all," he said with a feeble attempt at chivalry.

"I'm afraid I have. It's a long time and three children later."

"Two boys and a girl," Chet replied. "Mike, Todd, and—"

"—Katie," she said, her voice quivering. How incredible that he would know and remember her children's names. She embraced him. "Oh, Chet, I'm so sorry about Phyllis."

"At least she had you at the end. That means a lot to me. She was so fond of you," he said.

"Phyllis was a dear, wonderful person," Jane said honestly. Pulling away, she blinked back tears and said, "Oh, I'm sorry. This is my friend Shelley Nowack. Shelley, this is Chet Wagner and his son. John, we came over to go through Phyllis's belongings. They're almost all packed."

"Keep them, Jane," Chet said.

"Oh, no. I couldn't do that."

"It's what she'd want. It's what I want."

Jane caught a glimpse of John Wagner's surprised expression. Surprised and not at all pleased. "That's very nice of you, Chet, but we can talk about it later. I think in the meantime John ought to take the suitcases to his house. Just until things are settled."

They were all still standing around in front of the door. Nobody knew quite what to do next. This was probably Chet's house, legally, but he'd never been in it before. Shelley took things in hand. "I don't know where Bobby's gotten to. He was here when we came in. Why don't we all sit down?" Assuming the hostess role with a heavy-handed firmness, she shepherded everyone into the dining room, there still being no living room furniture. She and Jane hastily cleared away the rubble on the big table.

They were barely seated when there was the sound of a door opening somewhere else in the house and a toilet flushing. *The nasty jerk,* Jane thought. He probably hadn't even used the toilet, just flushed it to make a rude noise. A moment later, Bobby ambled into the room and stood leaning negligently against the dining room door frame. "Company's come, huh? Hi, John. Hi, Chet."

There was a stunned silence for a minute, then Chet stood up. Color had come to his face, and he suddenly seemed the "leader of industry" the press called him. Jane was astonished at the degree and suddenness of the change. "Don't you 'Chet' me, boy," he said in a ringing tone that all but knocked Jane back in her chair. "I'm certainly not your friend, and you can no longer claim the most tenuous relationship with me or my family. I'm Mr. Wagner to you, you punk."

For once, Bobby seemed shaken out of his in-control, arrogant pose. "But Phyllis was my mother, Chet."

"A biological accident. Nothing more. You had no claim on her, and you most assuredly have none on me. The only time I ever want to hear about you again is when I read in the newspaper that you've been duly convicted of her murder."

"Me? Get off it, Chet. I seen the news tonight. You're the one gonna fry for that."

John Wagner, silent until now, suddenly rose and, muttering incoherently, lunged at Bobby. But Chet was faster. He grabbed his son's arm. "Don't touch the slimy little bastard. We'll just let the lawyers fuck him over. That's what they're paid for. Excuse me, ladies. . . ."

Jane had an hysterical urge to giggle at the absurd incongruity of his apologizing for his language under the circumstances. She was surprised that he even remembered she and Shelley were present. She was also quite appalled that they *were* present. Intellectual snooping was one thing, but they had no business in the middle of a private emotional crisis like this. Coming to this house had been one of her bigger mistakes. These men were on the brink of violence, and Jane was terrified of what might happen. For the first time, it really came home to her that it was very likely one of these men was a murderer. And she and Shelley were witnessing something they shouldn't. But she was like an animal caught in the headlights of an oncoming car— horrified but unable to move.

Bobby seemed to feel he'd gained the upper hand again. "We'll see who's fucked over when Phyl's will turns up."

"Will? My wife's will is in the safe deposit box with mine, and I can assure you it's none of your concern," Chet said.

"I don't mean the old one. I mean the one she had made when we stopped off in New York the other day."

"You're lying!" John Wagner exclaimed.

"We'll see, won't we? She hauled me along to meet some old lawyer, then she went into his office and came out puttin' this blue folder thing in her purse."

"And where is this 'blue folder thing'? " Chet asked. His voice was so cold and malevolent that Jane involuntarily shivered. Didn't the stupid boy know when he was up against a formidable enemy? She'd run for the nearest bomb shelter if Chet Wagner ever spoke to her like that.

Apparently it didn't faze Bobby. He shrugged elaborately. "I got no idea. It's not here. She probably put it in the mail or something. It'll turn up, and believe me, you'll be eating your own shit when it does."

"Just what's that supposed to mean?" John asked. His face was flushed and blotched with fury. Jane was half afraid he was about to have a stroke.

"Figure it out yourself," Bobby said. Was it a bluff, or did he know what the will contained? Jane wondered. For that matter, was the whole story a bluff? She suspected it was. Phyllis wasn't the sort to even think about things likes wills—unless, of course, a greedy son reminded her.

"Oh, I'll figure it out," Chet was saying. "And first thing in the morning, I'll also figure out about this house. You better start your packing, boy, because you're going to be out of it. I curse the day I ever went looking for you. Phyllis would be alive today if I hadn't. I can never absolve myself of that."

The gentle emotion in his last words broke the spell Jane had been under. Barely able to get her breath, she rose quickly. "I have to go home. Shelley, help me finish the packing, will you?"

The two of them fled up the stairs. Raised voices followed them. Jane was cursing herself. They should have gotten out of the house. What misguided, ingrained sense of courtesy and obligation had made them rush to finish this appalling job? As they flung the last of Phyllis's belongings into the suitcases with little care, Shelley said in a trembling voice, "Dear God, if they're going to kill each other, let us get out of here first."

As she spoke, there was the sound of the front door slamming. For a moment Jane thought it was a gunshot, and she clung to Shelley's arm. But seconds later there was the sound of the Jaguar starting up. "They must have run him out for the time being. Shelley, I'm so sorry I got us into the middle of this."

"Don't you be sorry. It was my fault for asking you to do this," John Wagner said from the doorway.

"I was glad to do what little I could," Jane said, snapping shut the latch on the suitcase. John picked it and the other largest one up. Jane took the smaller ones, and Shelley went to the closet and took out Phyllis's mink jacket and purse.

John looked at the small, flat purse for a second, then set the cases down and took it from Shelley. He opened it and peered in. Jane was quite close and could see as well as he that there was no "blue folder thing" in it.

Still shaky and frantic to get away, they hauled everything downstairs and left it by the front door where John Wagner could easily take it to his car later. Chet, deflated, was still sitting at the dining room table with his head in his hands. He pulled himself together with a visible effort and insisted once again that Jane take Phyllis's things. And again, she demurred. "You'll let me know about the funeral, won't you?" she asked him as she edged toward the doorway.

"We'll be making the arrangements in the morning. Give me your address, and I'll come by."

"I won't be home most of tomorrow. I'll be at the house next door to here—" She gestured toward the Howards' house. "There's a church bazaar I'm helping set up."

After a few more awkward parting remarks, Jane and Shelley made their escape. They practically ran to the car and didn't even talk on the way home. There was too much to say but no way to say it.

Though the evening had seemed to last forever, it was only eight when Jane got home. She called Uncle Jim back.

"I didn't find out much, but Janey, if you're this Chet's friend, you're not gonna like this. Just a minute—" She could hear him rattling papers and could picture him fitting his bifocals on the end of his nose.

"Apparently his wife had left him and had come to Chicago to stay with a friend—you. Incidentally, that's the only mention of you I found. VanDyne was pulling your leg about you being a suspect. The husband flew in yesterday afternoon, called his office without mentioning where he was calling from, registered under the name Chester Weber at a hotel downtown. He rented a car, which he took out around midnight. It has enough miles on it to have gone to the house where his wife was staying and back, plus half a dozen miles. The lot is unattended after midnight, so nobody knows when he got back.''

Jane gulped, thinking about the two Chets she'd seen that night; one a broken husband and the other a ruthless businessman. "Still, none of that is proof, is it?"

"No, that's why he's not in jail. He claims he was distraught over his wife's departure. That he didn't think she'd really leave, but when she did, he followed her here with the intention of patching things up. Once he got to Chicago, he says he had second thoughts, decided to wait a few days and see if she'd come looking for him. That's why he says he used the false name and didn't tell his people where he was—to make her wonder and stew a bit if she did try to get in touch with him.''

"Where did he go when he went out so late?"

"That depends on your viewpoint. The investigators think he went to bump off his wife. He says he couldn't sleep and just went for an aimless drive.''

"That could be true, Uncle Jim.''

"Sure it could.''

"What about the murder weapon?''

"A kitchen knife from a set the victim had delivered with a bunch of other kitchen stuff that afternoon. No prints.''

"Could a killer have counted on a weapon being handy?''

"No, not unless he lived in the house or was visiting when the stuff came. If not, he probably had something of his own along in case there wasn't something sharp handy.''

"What about footprints," Jane asked. "There's a little snow on the ground.''

Jane could hear Uncle Jim shuffling some papers. "Let's see. Prints. A muddle of them going back and forth through the side yard from the house next door—''

"Yes, that was Albert Howard showing her the house."

"—a set coming to the front door, which were discovered to have gone clear down the block, door to door. Salesman or mail carrier or somebody. Another set of two children cutting across the backyard and peeping in a window. Window undamaged. And one set from the house on the other side that wandered around and got close but not clear up to the house."

"That's Mr. Finch, snooping."

"It looks like that's all he did, unless he could spring over a bush ten feet from the house. Your VanDyne had a few critical remarks about him in the report but no suggestions that he was responsible. A regular herd of prints run from the driveway to the front door. Presumably the people who moved all the furniture and whatnot in, plus the woman herself and her son. There's no sorting them out."

"Did Chet know where Phyllis was staying?"

"I didn't think to ask that. I would think he did or could have known. He called in to his office late in the afternoon, after she'd given orders to buy it."

"It still wouldn't be proof of his guilt. Uncle Jim, what's going to happen with all this conjecture?"

"They're either going to solve it, or they won't. It's that simple."

"You mean they might *never* figure out who did it?"

"Not quite. See, Janey, knowing who did it and accumulating enough verifiable evidence to bring to trial is a different matter. That would take a confession if nothing else turns up in the way of proof of guilt."

"But Phyllis can't go unavenged. She didn't deserve to be murdered."

"Lots of people don't deserve it, but it happens. Listen, Janey, you leave the avenging part to the police. You stay out of this. I'll keep you informed of everything I can find out, but in return, you keep your distance. Somebody didn't much mind killing her and probably wouldn't mind getting you out of the way if you butt in.''

"Okay—" she said, hoping that didn't count as a promise. "Thanks, Uncle Jim.''

The kids started coming home a few minutes later. Jane listened to Mike's story about the band director nearly having a breakdown at band practice and felt a deep sympathy with the man. She listened to Katie's half hour account of the fashion show and then helped Todd with his math homework. When they'd all gone to bed, she treated herself to a cigarette and a Coke, then checked for the third time that all the doors were locked before she settled down to watch *It's a Wonderful Life* on the late movie and crochet like crazy until midnight.

——17——

"Hey, Mom, that's pretty," Katie deigned to comment as she destroyed the living room looking for her missing social studies book the next morning. "Is it done?"

Jane studied the afghan spread across the back of the sofa. The twelve oversized granny squares were all done and put together. It actually looked as if someone who knew how to crochet had made them, she thought proudly. "No, it gets about four rows of solid stuff around the entire outside edge, but I don't know how to do the corners."

"Good-O, Mom. I think we ought to keep it," Mike said, joining Jane as she and Katie admired the work.

"I think so, too, but I promised it for the bazaar."

"Then buy it yourself."

She looked at him. "You mean, pay for the yarn, do all that work, and pay to buy it besides?"

"You did that last year with that wreath thing."

"Last year—" She stopped herself from saying: Last year your father was alive, and I wasn't worried about money. "I guess I did, didn't I? You ready to go? Is Todd on his way down?"

This was one of the horrible mornings when Jane drove all three kids' car pools to school. Just as there were occasional days when she got off scot-free, there were many more when she felt she was driving every

135

child in the county and ought to just buy a school bus and be done with it. She tried to arrange it so these days fell, like this one did, on Fridays. While it was true that the kids were hyper on Fridays, thereby increasing the risk of permanent injury to the driver's nervous system, they were at least happy-hyper, which was far nicer than Monday mornings when they all acted like she was driving them up to the front door of the guillotine.

She got Mike and his crowd of friends delivered to the high school, Katie and her car pool (not friends—a purely geographical arrangement made by Jane and the other mothers, which Katie mentioned critically nearly every morning) to the junior high, and Todd and his bunch to the grade school. Then she came home and collapsed at the kitchen table with a cup of coffee and the last few minutes of the *Today* show.

After watching about ninety seconds of a feature on a woman who was the mother of six adopted children (three with severe disabilities), who worked as a madly successful criminal lawyer and had invented (in her spare time, they said—*what* spare time?) some sort of toy that was supposed to rival the Hula Hoop, Jane flipped the television off in disgust. That sort of programming ought to be censored before impressionable young girls saw it and thought such a life was actually possible and/or required of them.

"I wonder what happens on the days when four of the kids are sick and a trial is supposed to start. . . ." she said aloud to Willard, who thumped his tail happily in response. "Probably uses some of that toy money to call in a squadron of babysitters."

As she opened pet food cans, she dialed Shelley's number. "What time are we supposed to go to Fiona's to start setting up?"

"Ten."

"Will you have time before then to show me how to finish the afghan?"

Shelley turned up a few minutes later, gave Jane her instructions, and sat down to watch her work. "Have you been thinking about last night?"

"I've been trying not to. Oh, Shelley, I finally understand that phrase about being of two minds. Every time somebody starts going on about how much Phyllis thought of me, I feel like I ought to dash out and start interrogating people myself because of this tremendous emotional debt I didn't even know I had. Did you notice that even Chet knew my kids' names? *That*'s how much she talked about me. But then I pull myself together and realize there could be a hundred explanations for all this that I know nothing about. I mean, what do I really know about Phyllis's life? Nothing. Chet could have some deadly enemy who killed Phyllis to get at him. For that matter, Bobby probably has perfectly awful chums in the city who were just waiting for him to get back, and one of them might have killed Phyllis by mistake. The worst is, I don't really believe the police will ever unravel it. I talked to Uncle Jim last night—"

She proceeded to tell Shelley about the conversation.

"So the evidence all points to Chet?" Shelley said when she was done.

"No, just the circumstances. There isn't any evidence to speak of. And I wouldn't think much more is likely to turn up, unless someone has a violent attack of conscience and confesses," Jane said.

"So you still don't think it's Chet?"

"I don't want to think so. Didn't you see how devastated he was by it all?"

"I did. And I also saw how he pulled himself out of it in seconds to confront Bobby. It was almost like watching a multiple personality kick in."

"Kinda spooky, wasn't it?"

"That's putting it mildly. I think the one person most capable of violence, from what we saw last night, is John Wagner. If his father hadn't stopped him, I think he'd have reduced Bobby to a grease spot without a second thought," Shelley said.

"Could you blame him?"

"Not a bit."

"But I still can't imagine anybody working up that kind of animosity toward Phyllis. Poor Phyllis. What do you think?"

"I think we better get over to Fiona's and concentrate on getting the bazaar set up."

Jane bundled up the afghan so Willard wouldn't sleep on it and sighed. "Did I actually volunteer for this, or is it all just a nightmare?"

"Both."

Jane went to her kitchen radio and tuned in an FM station that played Christmas music. "Why turn that on? We're leaving," Shelley said.

"Partly so it's playing when I get home, and partly— I know this sounds dumb—so that the sound will soak into the house."

"Do you think if you create enough atmosphere, a tree, complete with decorations, will appear in your living room?"

Jane laughed. "Anything's possible."

The nightmare qualities of the Christmas craft bazaar became more apparent when they got to Fiona's. The rental company that was supposed to deliver the folding display tables at eight hadn't arrived yet. "I've called three times already," Fiona said, her usual English calm, if not shattered, at least crumbling around the edges. "They swear they're on the way and we're the first delivery."

"Then there's nothing we can do?" Jane asked. She had hopes that she could escape and go home to get in a few more frantic minutes of crocheting.

"Wrong!" Shelley exclaimed. "We can start pricing. It's the worst job of all."

"There are degrees of worseness in this?" Jane asked.

Fiona laughed. She had a delightful, bubbly laugh that broke the tension. "Let's get it over with."

"Fiona, you really don't have to help," Jane assured her. "When you offered your house, we swore you wouldn't have to do anything else."

"Jane, have you gone mad?" Shelley asked. "If you start turning down offers to help, I'll just have to slap some sense back into you. Let's start with . . ." She looked around the room full of boxes, and her shoulders sagged. ". . . with the pillows. They were purchased; we just have to figure out the markup. No personalities involved."

Jane soon discovered what the remark about personalities meant. Many of the volunteers who had provided sale items had affixed a suggested price. These prices were almost universally inflated beyond reason. Someone had sent over a box of flower paintings done on wooden shingles. While not great art by any means, they weren't bad, and Jane felt she could probably find some out of the way wall in her house where one might fit nicely—until she noticed the note saying they should be priced at forty dollars each.

"Forty dollars!" she exclaimed, clutching at her heart. "I was thinking seven or eight."

Shelley, her head buried in a box, emerged. "Oh, those. That's easy. The woman who does those always comes first thing in the morning to see if we've marked them right. As soon as she goes, we mark them down to something reasonable. She's never caught on yet.

She makes them every year, and they go like hotcakes at five dollars.''

''What about these?'' Jane had opened a dress box full of little wreaths. They were green yarn crocheted in a sort of ruffle on a curtain rod ring. With the addition of bright red sequins and a tiny satin bow, they made nice little ornaments. But a note in the box said: ''I saw these for sale in New York last year for fifteen dollars. I think ten would be reasonable, don't you?''

Shelley came over to look at the wreaths and then at the signature on the note. ''That's a bit tricky. She's a big contributor to the church, and we don't want to piss her off.''

Fiona looked over her shoulder. ''Oh, she's out of town. When she brought the box over she mentioned that she was going to see her son in Hawaii for the holidays and was leaving today.''

''Terrific. They'll really move at two dollars.''

''Isn't that a truck I hear?'' Fiona exclaimed.

It took until noon to get the tables in and arranged. The women, including Suzie Williams, who had arrived just behind the rental company truck, then set about making a rough arrangement. Suzie favored logic and order. ''Put all the pillows and quilts in one room, all the food stuff in another—''

''I'm not sure,'' Shelley said. ''If a person on a diet sees a room full of food, she might just give it all a miss. Same with people who don't like 'loving hands from home' art. You want to take them by surprise.''

''That makes sense. Trick them into buying shit they don't want,'' Suzie gave in cheerfully.

''Let's take a break,'' Fiona suggested. Jane had the feeling that Suzie's raw language offended their hostess, though Fiona was always gracious to her. ''I fixed some chicken salad and fresh banana bread this morning."

They settled in around the big kitchen table. "Where's your husband today? Hiding from us?" Suzie asked. She'd long been fascinated by the idea of a husband who did his work—whatever work, if any, he did—at home.

"Upstairs. He's got a miserable headache," Fiona replied. She set out everyday plates that Jane would have kept in a safe deposit box if they'd been hers. "When he was a boy, he had a bad fall from a tree and got a skull fracture. It all healed perfectly well, but he still gets these occasional headaches that devastate him. The doctors seem to think there's a connection, but there's nothing to do about it."

Suzie nodded knowingly. "I broke my ankle when I was ten, and it still hurts sometimes. Oh, music—how nice."

They all fell silent. There was music playing somewhere, and as they listened, it became recognizable.

Richie Divine's "Red Christmas."

Jane glanced at Fiona, who had become quite pale and was looking toward the glass patio doors leading to the backyard.

"Where's it coming from?" Suzie asked, as yet blissfully unaware of the tension in the room.

Shelley rose and went to the doors. As she opened one, a blast of cold air and a blast of music came in together. "It's coming from outside," she said softly.

Fiona rose slowly and joined her at the door. Jane and Suzie followed her. As she listened, Jane knew exactly where it was coming from—the deck of the house next door. Phyllis's house. Now Bobby's. That elaborate sound system was rigged so the speakers could sit on the deck outside the master bedroom.

But why annoy the Howards?

Suddenly Albert Howard appeared in the kitchen doorway behind the four women. ''What the hell is that noise?'' he asked.

18

Albert disappeared and Fiona, white faced, ran after him. Try as they might, Shelley, Jane, and Suzie could hear nothing of what they were saying to each other.

"Is that the little fart next door playing the music? The one whose mother was a friend of yours?" Suzie asked Jane, when Albert and Fiona had moved out of earshot.

"I'm afraid so, but I don't get it. Why is he trying to irritate the whole neighborhood, and why—of all things—a Richie Divine record?"

"Why not?" Suzie asked, then said, "Oh, yeah. I forgot Fiona was married to him, wasn't she? Or is that just a typical neighborhood rumor?"

"No, it's true," Jane said. "That room through there is full of his stuff. Pictures, gold records."

"The one Fiona didn't want us to use? Oh, well, it's probably just coincidence that the kid is playing that record. I heard it on the car radio on the way over. It's played a lot this time of year."

"Still, what's the point, aside from making sure nobody misses the fact that he's a nasty little bastard?" Shelley asked, closing the door and shooing them back to the kitchen table. "Let's eat lunch and act like we don't hear it. For Fiona's sake."

"I always enjoy it when I can eat for someone else's sake," Suzie said, serving herself a large dollop of chicken salad. "The calories don't count that way. Just like they don't count if you eat them before seven in the morning or on a holiday—national or religious. I'm not sure about state holidays."

"I wish my thighs observed those rules," Jane said, helping herself to some food. "Wow, this is terrific. It's got little green grapes in it. Where do you suppose she gets such nice ones this time of year?"

"Sorts them out of cans of fruit salad?" Suzie suggested.

Fiona rejoined them a few minutes later, looking as cool and unruffled as the proverbial cucumber. The music was still audible, but they all pretended they didn't notice. "Albert so seldom tries to take a nap in the middle of the day. He gets positively savage when someone interrupts it," was her only comment. "Have some more banana bread, ladies. If you leave any, I'll eat it all, and you'll have to roll me out of this chair."

Doggedly ignoring the music—it wasn't the single, it was the whole *Richie Divine's Greatest Hits* album— they finished lunch and went back to work. Fiona got busy shifting some of the tables into better positions and draping them with the rented white tablecloths. Suzie, under Shelley's direction, appointed herself to take each box to the room in which the contents would be sold. Shelley sat on the floor, making a rough sort of inventory of each item as Suzie took it away, and Jane started printing up prices on a sheet of sticky labels for the crocheted wreaths. "I think we ought to give one of these free to anybody who buys more than a certain amount," Jane said. "You could pin them on their coats as they go out the door."

"Good thinking. I'll put half of them by the cashier, and some people may pick them up as one last thing before their stuff is rung up."

"Impulse buying. Right."

"Oh, my God, will you look at this quilt," Shelley said. "It's gorgeous. And it's already marked at—at *twenty-five dollars!* That's criminal. It ought to be at least a hundred and fifty. Think how beautiful this would look in my guest room. I'm going to buy it myself for two hundred, but we'll hang it up marked SOLD, just because it's so pretty."

Jane tried hard not to give in to envy. Would she ever be able to impulsively buy anything for two hundred dollars? "Where should I put this jelly?" she asked.

Shelley turned on her. "Jelly?" she asked suspiciously. "Is it from Marijo Fisher?"

"Yes, what's wrong with that?"

"Oh, nothing, except it's Marijo's little ploy to rip us off every year. I thought I'd made clear to her that I wasn't letting her get away with it again."

"I don't get it. How does she rip us off with jelly? It looks good."

"Oh, it is good. It's fantastic. She sends over four or five piddling jars, then gives people delicious samples. Of course, the four or five jars are gone in no time, but samples keep miraculously appearing, and she takes orders for about a billion more."

"So?"

"Not for the bazaar fund, Jane. For herself. She earns the church ten bucks and a couple hundred later for herself. It infuriates me. Is her phone number on there? I'm going to have a word or two with her." She stormed off and returned a few minutes later looking like a general who's had an unusually good day crushing invading armies. "It's all taken care of," she said serenely.

Jane was afraid to ask.

After another ten minutes, Jane said, "Is that music as annoying to you as it is to me?"

"It isn't that loud. Imagine if it were spring and the

windows were open. Still, I wonder why nobody's called the police to make him shut it off.''

Fiona passed the doorway carrying a stack of linens and looking miserable.

''I'm not going to let him do this to her,'' Jane said. She threw on her coat and slipped out the front door before Shelley could reason with her. Stomping down the long drive, along the sidewalk, and up to the house next door, she leaned on the doorbell and knocked a few times for good measure.

Bobby came to the door wearing his usual smirk. ''Yeah?''

''I've come to ask you politely to turn off that music. If you don't, however, I'm going to have the police come and talk to you about it, Bobby.''

''It's a free country,'' he said as if he'd thought up the concept himself. ''Don't you like rock? Would you rather have a little Fred Waring?'' He sneered.

''I happen to like Fred Waring. And I also like Twisted Sister, but at a reasonable level and when I want to listen to it. Right now I don't think the whole neighborhood wants to let you make the choice for them. Turn it off!''

''I'll think about it,'' he said with an obnoxious chuckle before slamming the door in her face.

Jane got back to the Howards' house fueled by pure rage. ''If Phyllis is in heaven, she's probably still trying to explain herself for having given birth to such a monster!'' she said as Shelley opened the door to her. ''I'm calling the police on him.''

''Jane, I'm all for self-assertiveness, but I don't think it's smart to mess with that kid. He could be a murderer, you know.''

''Clear the way,'' a voice behind a vast stack of empty boxes said. It was Suzie. ''Get the door for me. I'm going to put these out in the garage.''

Jane and Shelley stood arguing halfheartedly for a minute more. Suzie came bounding back. "Hey, guys, you gotta see this."

Shelley grabbed her coat, and they followed Suzie along the path that ran between the Howards' house and Bobby's. Before they could see what was happening, they could hear the argument. Mr. Finch was standing at the front door, waving his arms and screaming unintelligibly in a high voice. They couldn't see Bobby, but they did see his fist suddenly pop out and catch Mr. Finch on the chin.

"Jane, *do* go call the police," Shelley said.

"And miss this? Not on your life," Jane replied.

Finch had tumbled into the snow but picked himself up with lightning speed and flung himself toward the door and out of sight. A second later, a bundle of humanity with four legs and four arms rolled down the steps and into the yard. They thrashed around ineffectually in the patchy snow for a moment, apparently not doing each other much harm. Just as Jane was about to give up watching and run for the phone, a siren wailed over the sound of Richie Divine's voice. Apparently someone else had seen the fight coming or had gotten fed up with the music.

A police car pulled to a sudden stop in front of the house, and two uniformed officers ran across the lawn and separated Bobby and Mr. Finch without too much difficulty. "Show's over, ladies," one of the officers called to them.

Jane blushed with embarrassment.

Suzie had a much higher embarrassment threshold. "Sonofabitch," she muttered with heat. The three of them hurried back to the house, and Suzie continued. "Couple of wimps. I could have beaten them both."

Fiona was at the door. "What in the world became of you?"

They told her about the fight.

"Oh, dear," Fiona said, sounding defeated. "This is all so unpleasant, and I hold myself to blame. If I hadn't mentioned that house was for sale, it would still be nice and vacant. What if something awful happens while the bazaar is going on? We can hardly expect people to pick their way through a full-scale battle to buy a few Christmas things."

"We'll worry about that if it happens," Shelley said briskly. "There won't be a bazaar if we don't get back to work."

Nothing more was heard from next door. The music stopped a few minutes after the police arrived. The four women worked in peace all afternoon. The only interruption was John Wagner dropping by to tell Jane that there would be a funeral service for his stepmother at ten o'clock the next morning. Fortunately, Fiona's maid, Celia, showed him in directly to where Jane was working, and he didn't cross paths with either Fiona or Albert.

"Dad thought about having her buried from the old church they went to when they lived in the city, but I talked him into having it out here." He made no reference to the events of the night before, and neither did Jane.

"Do you want me to come along to the funeral?" Shelley asked when he'd left.

"Good Lord, no! You promised to fight the crowds with me to do some Christmas shopping tomorrow afternoon. That's all anybody could ask of a friend."

"I'm *so* glad you realize that. Now, about pricing these fruitcakes—"

Shelley had to drive a car pool at three, Suzie at three-thirty, and Jane at three forty-five, but each returned to finish off one job or another. They sat down for a last slice of Fiona's banana bread and a cup of coffee at five, confident that they had the bazaar situation well in hand.

If only the rest of life could be handled by hard work and organization, Jane thought longingly. How unutterably sad that Phyllis couldn't have been with them. It was exactly the sort of day she'd have loved. What had Mel VanDyne been doing all day while they sorted and priced Christmas knickknacks? Jane wondered. Was he any closer to finding Phyllis's killer?

19

Jane got up Saturday morning far earlier than necessary. It was refreshing to enjoy the illusion of having the house to herself. The kids were all sleeping late, so she didn't have to worry about running out of hot water before she was through showering, about fighting Katie for the hot curlers, or about having to drop everything and drive somebody to school before she'd booted up her brain. No music blared from stereos, no cars honked impatiently in the driveway, nobody ran through the house wildly searching for lost books or lunch money or permission slips.

Bliss.

The first order of business was to get ready for Phyllis's funeral. She was going to wear her charcoal gray suit and black silk blouse. Shelley had bought it for her for Steve's funeral last winter, and this was the first time since then that she'd worn it. She got it out and put it on with a certain amount of dread. After all, the associations were grim. Yet she looked in the mirror and was surprised to see herself smiling a bit. This wasn't the same woman who wore the suit last February. That Jane had been blotto—emotionally and physically wiped out.

Everybody had been so sympathetic and mistaken then. That was the hardest part—to act the role of a woman who had lost her loving partner, when inside she was raging with rejection, furious at his disloyalty, and despising herself for her own stupidity and failure.

But this was a new woman wearing the charcoal suit. Under Shelley's dictatorial guidance, she'd streaked her hair, gone in for regular perms, lost a little weight, and learned a bit about makeup, although mascara still made her feel like she had raccoon eyes. "Eat your heart out, Steve," she told the mirror and felt a little tingle of vindication.

It was only eight-thirty when she went downstairs for a quiet hour of finishing up the afghan. While she was feeding the animals, she heard the soft purr of a car in the driveway and was surprised—and pleased, for once—to see the red MG. Imagine Mel VanDyne catching her at her best, instead of her worst. It might be a sign.

When she opened the front door to him, she was gratified to see the look on his face. "Mrs. Jeffry— Jane, I hope I'm not disturbing you," he said.

"Not at all. Come in." She led him to the living room, deliciously aware that he was staring at her. "Please, sit down. Could I get you anything? Coffee?"

"If you have a Coke around, I could use a caffeine fix."

"I can do better than that. The kids have something that's got tons of caffeine. It's advertised that way." She came back with a glass of ice and a can of something with a lightning bolt on the label.

He took a sip and grimaced happily. "If you don't mind my saying so, 'you look mauwvellous!' "

"Thanks," Jane said with a laugh. "Nice of you to notice. I know it's considered very old-fashioned to wear dark colors for funerals, but I just can't throw on a pink dress for one. My mother taught me too well."

"Does your mother live here?"

She wondered why he was being so chatty but decided not to look a gift horse in the mouth. "No, my mother lives all over the place. Right now she and my father are in a little country in Africa. They're State Department. My dad has a positively spooky gift for language. He can start speaking almost anything the day he first hears it, so they've spent their life all over the world, wherever our government wants to hear what's being said."

"Did you grow up that way?"

"Oh, yes. In fact, when my husband and I moved here, it was two years before I could bear to unpack the last suitcase and put it in the basement storage. Force of habit—I was so sure I would have to move again. What *are* you doing here this morning?"

She'd taken him off guard. "Why, I—I wondered if you wanted a ride to the funeral. No, that's not the truth. I wanted to ask you some questions, too."

"About what? I've already told you everything I know about Phyllis."

"It isn't about her." He paused a moment, then went on in a brisk, professional tone, "This morning, about five, when a trash-hauling company picked up their dumpster behind the shopping mall, there was a body beside it. Bobby's."

Jane felt her bright perkiness fade as if someone had thrown a bucket of cold water over her. "Oh, no. How did he die?"

"Stabbed. From behind. Somebody must have taken him completely by surprise."

"Behind a dumpster at the mall? What on earth was he doing there? Besides getting killed?"

"That's probably all. I imagine he was supposed to meet someone."

Mel was silent as Jane rummaged in the end table drawer until she found a stale cigarette. He leaned forward and lit it for her. She sat back and took a long drag. "It's odd," she finally said, sensing that he was waiting for her to say something. "I'm not surprised or sad, because he was probably the most hateful, obnoxious person I've ever known. But in another way, I am sorry. It's just not right to stab people in the back because they're awful."

"I've always sort of felt that way," he said wryly.

"It certainly blows my theory of Bobby being Phyllis's killer. Unless Chet—" She caught herself thinking out loud.

Mel VanDyne laughed at her discomfiture. "Do you honestly think that wouldn't occur to me? Don't be so careful what you don't say. It won't stop me from thinking, but what you *do* say could help."

"All right. Unless Chet killed him as revenge."

"I take it you've talked to Chet Wagner."

"Oh, yes—" Jane told him about the evening she and Shelley went over to pack Phyllis's things and found themselves in the midst of a dispute between Bobby and the Wagner father and son.

VanDyne was dumbfounded and displeased. "Why in the world didn't you ask an officer to go with you? You could have put yourselves in a dangerous situation."

"I don't know. It sounds a lot stupider now than it did at the time. I guess we just weren't thinking. Still, it was an interesting experience, to say the least."

"Did you get the feeling that Chet Wagner honestly believed Bobby was responsible for his mother's death?"

Jane thought for a long moment. "That's hard to say. I'm certain he held Bobby to blame for the *circumstances* which brought about her death, but to be honest, I think he'd have mauled him on the spot regardless of witnesses if he'd thought Bobby actually killed her.

He was furious, but it was Chet himself who kept John from attacking Bobby.''

"Did John Wagner think Bobby was responsible for her death? Is that why he tried to attack Bobby?''

"No, it was because Bobby said Chet was going to be blamed. I think he was outraged on his father's behalf, and of course Bobby had hit on his worst fear. Bobby was being absolutely revolting.''

"Hmmm. Tell me again about this will business. When I inquired, Mr. Wagner said his will and his wife's were with a lawyer on the island, and he authorized us to request a photocopy. It should be here today. He seemed quite cool about it. Of course, that was before Bobby dropped his bombshell.''

"But if there was another more recent will, the earlier one wouldn't be valid anyway. Actually, I'm not at all sure it wasn't all bluff, just to further insult Chet. The only convincing part of it was that he said she came out of the lawyer's office with a 'blue folder thing' she was putting in her purse. That sounded true, or at least possible. I don't think he had the wit or imagination to make up convincing little details like 'blue' and 'folder.' He'd have just said 'papers' if he was making it up, I think. I knew a girl in school who was a really good liar, and she got away with it because there were always all kinds of tiny, vivid, believable details in her stories. You bought the details, and before you realized it, you'd bought the whole story.''

"I think that's characteristic," Mel said shortly.

Jane realized she'd been wandering off the main point again, a habit that annoyed him. "However, there wasn't a will or anything that looked like one in her things," she continued. "We went through everything—not snooping—well, yes, snooping—and the only paperwork was in a needlepointed case. One envelope in there contained memorabilia. Family pictures, high school yearbook, birth certificates, that sort of thing. The other envelope was all craft stuff. Patterns, order forms from yarn shops.''

"Yes, I saw that.''

"I thought you probably had. Her purse, too?''

"Yes. There wasn't anything incriminating in it. If there actually had been a will and she'd had it in her purse in New York, where could it have gone? Was it a direct flight, or did they go someplace else on the way here?''

"I believe it was direct. She could have put it in a safe deposit box there or mailed it to someone.''

"She could, but why would she?''

There was another long silence before Jane said, "Hadn't we better get going? Did you mean it about driving me to the funeral, or was that just a ploy to catch me off guard so I'd burst into hysterical tears and admit to killing Bobby?''

"I've got better ploys than that. Yes, I meant it.''

Jane went up and told a very sleepy Mike that she was leaving. Once in Mel's car, she was glad—for a change—that she wasn't tall and leggy. She'd have had her knees up around her ears if she were. "What do you know about Bobby's death? Weapon, that sort of thing?'' she asked him when they were under way.

"Next to nothing. He must have gotten a call or made some arrangement to meet someone there. We didn't have the phone tapped—an oversight, damn it all. He was stabbed. The weapon removed from the scene. It probably happened between one and four in the morning.''

"No better clues than that?''

"Afraid not. Jane, this was too late for the morning papers, and I'm assuming nobody but the murderer knows about it yet, so I don't want you to say anything about it at the funeral.''

Jane felt deflated. "I get it. I'm an excuse for you to be there observing how everybody's behaving."

He put his gloved hand over hers for a second. "Only partly, Jane."

She gazed out the window. Mother always said, "Half a loaf is better than none." But this was the soggy bottom half; she wanted the crusty, buttery top half.

─── 20 ───

If Mel VanDyne had expected emotional fireworks at the funeral, he was disappointed. The widower behaved with cool decorum. John Wagner stayed close to his father, looking vaguely belligerent but otherwise no more upset than any stepson who was only slightly fond of his late stepmother. Jane noticed both of them casting a quick eye over the assembly once or twice, but whether they were looking for Bobby or merely curious about who was in attendance, it was impossible to say. John sat next to his father, and on his other side there was a mousy woman Jane remembered from volleyball days, presumably the downtrodden Joannie. Beside her there was a lean, red-headed man in his thirties who leaned across Joannie and whispered to John a couple of times. Jane assumed that he was the brother from the London office.

Closest to the family were a number of muscular, stern-faced young men. Jane realized that they must be bodyguards. Of course a man of Chet's money and international standing must have them, so why did she find their presence so foreign and alarming? Other than the family and the bodyguards, the funeral was well attended by a lot of extremely well-heeled people, presumably Chet's wealthy friends who had flocked in from whatever fashionable watering holes they normally frequented. The women's clothes were magnificent, and the men all looked like aging movie stars. Jane tried to picture Phyllis socializing with these people and failed.

Next in the pecking order were the small legion of people she assumed were Chet's staff and business associates. They were identifiable by their yuppie looks and fawning demeanors.

There wasn't a tear in the crowd. If anyone genuinely grieved for Phyllis—besides Chet—they were keeping it well hidden. Jane sat listening to the bland service, obviously conducted for a woman none of them knew well, and tried to find a feeling of true loss somewhere in her own heart. All she found was guilt.

The only interesting part of the ordeal, as far as Jane was concerned, was the fact that a couple of network news crews had gathered outside the church during the service. Chet, John, John's wife, Joannie, and the redheaded Wagner son had taken places with the minister at the door of the church in a sort of reverse receiving line. Being in the back row, Jane was among the first out. As Chet opened the door for her, a cameraman leaped into action, focusing on Jane as she came down the steps clutching Mel's arm to keep from taking a header on the icy steps.

Accustomed to cameras, VanDyne snarled, "Buzz off, boys," and shoved her unceremoniously through the crowd and into the red MG.

"Andy Warhol promised me fifteen minutes of fame," Jane mused as they roared off. "I wonder if it's all going to be in five-second intervals. Did you learn anything?"

"Not a damned thing. They didn't even seem to notice that he was missing."

"They were all probably too relieved to question a good thing."

"Jane, do you mind if I drop you off at home? I've

got to get back to the coroner and see what he's found out.''

''Far be it from me to keep a man from his coroner,'' Jane said. Did he mean he would have otherwise offered her lunch or something semidatish?

When he'd left, she called Shelley. ''I saw you come back with VanDyne,'' her friend said. ''You look smashing, by the way. Want to go someplace fancy for lunch before deterioration starts to set in?''

''I'd love it. Shelley, Bobby was murdered overnight.''

''I know. Suzie told me.''

''It wasn't even in the paper. How did Suzie know?''

''She had to run down to the mall early this morning to set up for a lingerie sale. It was the talk of the town. Who did it? Why there? When? Where do we send our thank-you notes?''

''Shelley, you don't mean that.''

''I know I don't. But he's a hard person to feel sorry about. Was the funeral hideous? What about lunch? We can pick the whole case apart.''

Over crab quiche and white wine, Jane told Shelley what little she knew about Bobby's death. ''So nothing at the scene helped them?'' Shelley asked.

''Apparently not. Unless VanDyne is concealing information from me—which is entirely possible. The only reason he was being chummy with me was so he could go to the funeral 'disguised' as a friend of a friend of the family. Shelley, there *is* such a thing as an unsolved crime—''

''Probably many more of them than we're led to believe,'' Shelley agreed.

''I have this awful feeling Bobby and Phyllis are going to end up in that category. The thing that scares me is the thought that whoever killed them may not be through.'' She took a last bite of her quiche. ''Suppose it was somebody like Mr. Finch—not that I think it was—but if he killed them for something he imagined was an insult to him, he might just go right on and bump off Fiona or somebody. On the other hand, suppose it was Chet or John Wagner—''

''Then it's a domestic matter, not likely to go any further,'' Shelley said firmly.

''Not necessarily. If one of them did it, they might think somebody else had a clue—maybe even us—and is a danger to their getting away with it.''

''Us? What do we know?''

Jane paused. ''We might know lots of things we don't realize are significant.''

Shelley waited while the waiter came and took their plates and dessert orders. When he'd gone, she crossed her arms and leaned forward. ''Jane, what's on your mind?''

Jane lowered her voice. ''Shelley, this little memory jiggled through my mind during the service. Remember when Chet and John came over that night and we went to the door because Bobby didn't? Picture what happened.''

Shelley frowned. ''Nothing happened. They came in the door. That's all.''

''No, they came in a locked door . . .''

Shelley leaned back in her chair. ''. . . that *we* didn't open.''

''Right. *John Wagner had a key.*''

The waiter hovered until they were done and the shopping mall was too crowded for further conversation. They left the restaurant, and Jane got out a little notebook she carried in her purse. ''Let's see. I've got Mike's CDs to get and something for Thelma and Dixie Lee. That ought to finish it up.''

"You're not buying Mike a CD player, are you?"

"Good Lord, no! I can't afford a thing like that. Thelma's getting it. I hate for her to give the kids such expensive gifts. She only does it to put me in a bad light."

"Come on, Jane. That's not fair. They're her only grandchildren, and she's got plenty of money to spend, so why shouldn't she?"

"Yes, you're right. But I wish Steve's brother Ted and his wife, Dixie Lee, would get on with having kids, so she could disperse her interest a little. I should be grateful she didn't buy Mike a car. I was afraid she was going to."

"All right. Let's get the CDs first," Shelley said, glaring dangerously at a group of women who had jostled her.

Standing over a rack full of Billy Joel CDs, and finding themselves momentarily alone, Shelley said, "There are lots of reasons he could have had a key. Phyllis might have given it to him. She probably did."

"Yes—it's not really the key itself that's bothering me. I just meant it was something like that. Or several somethings skittering through my brain— Shelley," she gasped, "do you know what these things *cost?*"

After purchasing four of the shiny plastic disks, they moved on to a luggage store, where Shelley knew there was a sale on extremely good, frumpy handbags. That took care of Jane's mother-in-law. "She'll just take it back," Jane groused.

"Of course she will, but she might apply the credit to a suitcase and then get the urge to go on a trip. You can't lose."

"Oh, Shelley, you are a comfort to me!" Jane said with a laugh.

A matched set of necklace, earrings, and bracelet in very good mock turquoise and silver let Jane mark her sister-in-law's name off her list. "That's really pretty stuff," Jane said. "I can't believe they aren't hot at that price. She'll love them. So would I. If Steve were alive, I'd go home and hint like mad. You know, it's very strange not shopping for him. I actually put his name on my list when I started this and felt like a fool."

"Old habits," Shelley said astringently. "Let's get on our way. I'm getting claustrophobic."

On the way home, they chewed over the business of John Wagner having a key but came to no clear conclusion, except that Jane really ought to at least mention it to Mel VanDyne. It had seemed a long day already, and Jane felt her brain turning to mush. Once home, she hid her purchases and put the roast into the oven. It had been marinating for two days in wine vinegar, cloves, and onions and smelled good enough to eat raw. It was Uncle Jim's favorite dinner, and if he was going to drive clear out to the suburbs, which he hated, to sit through a band concert, a good dinner was the least she could do for him.

After touching base with each of the kids, she went to her room, took off her suit, silk blouse, and panty hose, and lay down for a short nap. But her mind kept wandering around the question of the murders. She *knew* something important, she was sure of it, but she couldn't land squarely on what it was. It was something she'd noticed recently.

Something she'd seen . . .

"What a very *interesting* seasoning," Thelma Jeffry said with critical reflection as she chewed on a bit of roast beef.

Uncle Jim winked at Jane. "It's German, Thelma," he said. "When Jane's family and I lived in West Berlin, her mother fixed this nearly every Sunday just for me."

"Jane, I didn't know you lived there—too." She made it sound like they were gypsies who'd called a painted wagon their home. "Such a dangerous place to take children, I would have thought."

"Not really," Jane said breezily. "My sister and I used to play hide-and-seek on the Berlin Wall. The guards were really nice. Especially the Russian ones."

Thelma gasped and looked like she wanted to clamp her hands over the children's ears to keep them from hearing about their mother's foolishness.

"I'm joking, Thelma," Jane told her reluctantly. "My sister and I weren't born then, and The Wall didn't exist. Mike, would you please join us?"

Throughout the meal Mike had been rehearsing for the upcoming concert. Tapping his foot to the beat of music none of them could hear, he was intently practicing his fingering on his milk glass. He hadn't spoken throughout the whole meal.

"Huh? Oh, Mom, you did get the oil and water checked and put some air in the tires, didn't you?"

"Mike, it's only a few blocks," she said, passing him the potatoes. "Mike is driving himself tonight," she explained to the rest of them.

"First time out on the new driver's license?" Uncle Jim asked.

"Oh, Jane, do you *really* think that's a good idea?" Thelma asked.

"No, I'm quite certain it's not. I don't think he should drive until he's at least twenty-five. But the state of Illinois says it is, and he passed his test with flying colors—and I do mean flying!"

"Mike, why don't you let me take you and your friends in my Lincoln?" Thelma offered.

Mike looked so stricken at the idea of showing up at the school being driven by his grandmother that Jane took pity. She wouldn't just take him, she'd go in with him and want to fuss around straightening his collar and taking dozens of pictures. "No, Thelma, I promised Mike he could drive himself. He needs to be there earlier than the rest of us."

"I know what Steve would have thought," Thelma said repressively.

"Maybe you don't," Jane replied, knowing better but unable to stop herself. "I wonder if you ever knew about the time Steve went to Michigan when he was thirteen and drove your car around all weekend? He told me many times what fun it was."

This exaggeration of a story Steve had mentioned only once reduced Thelma to a sputtering simmer that lasted through the meal. When Mike finally got ready to go, Jane went to the driveway with him, despite his efforts to leave without fanfare. She grabbed his arm as he started to get in the car. "Honey, I know you don't want to hear this or need to hear it, but I have to say it: drive carefully.''

To her astonishment, he gave her a big hug. "Thanks, Mom, and thanks, too, for keeping Gramma off my tail.''

"I love you, Mike.''

"And I love you, Mom, but the guys are waiting. Remember, you promised not to look at the program or let anybody tell you what we play last. It's a surprise you'll like.''

She stood back and wiped the back of her hand across her eyes. Hugging herself and shivering in the cold, she stood her ground until the taillights of the station wagon were out of sight. It was all she could do to keep from running down the street shouting, "Come back. Come back. Stay my little boy. Please don't grow up!''

When she came back in the house, Thelma started to say something, and Jane heard Uncle Jim rumble quietly, "Leave her alone, Thelma.''

After a quiet little cry in the guest bathroom, Jane washed her face and emerged to serve dessert. Uncle Jim's warning had worked. Thelma didn't even comment on the fact that all the Christmas decorations were up, but the presents were sitting in a heap in the corner of the room, waiting for a tree to arrive.

When dinner was over, they organized themselves to go to the concert. Todd was a bit slow getting himself together, but Katie was waiting at the door, fidgeting with impatience. "What's with you?'' Jane asked. "I've never known you to be eager to go to a band concert.''

"I like 'em, Mom. And besides, there's this really neat guy playing with the junior high orchestra I want to show you.''

"Of course there is. Why did I have to ask?" Jane said with a smile.

"I think you really ought to get Mike his own car," Katie said, trailing her to the closet. "I mean, he's got a job and school and band, and you're always having to drive him someplace, and think how much easier it would be for you if he could take himself. And you would still have your car to go wherever you wanted."

Jane slipped on her coat and fished in the pockets for her gloves. "I didn't come to town on a turnip truck, kiddo."

"What do you mean by that?"

"Just that I know exactly what this excess of consideration for Mike and me is all about. If I were to get Mike a car when he's sixteen, you'd be in a position to say I should get you one when you turn sixteen. Otherwise, it wouldn't be fair. Right?"

Katie grinned. "It can't hurt to try. That's what you always say."

Thelma insisted on taking her car and commandeered Katie and Todd to ride with her, a plan that was just fine with Jane. It gave her a short time alone with Uncle Jim. Of unspoken accord, neither of them had mentioned the murders in Thelma's presence. Jane was surprised the subject hadn't come up, but apparently Thelma's eagle eye for bad news had missed them altogether, or she'd failed to make the neighborhood connection.

Unfortunately, Jane's hurried and intensive questioning during the short ride to the school auditorium didn't provide her with any useful information. Uncle Jim had not only snooped into the file on Phyllis's death, he'd even called VanDyne and chatted with him about it. He'd also looked over the reports on Bobby's murder. All of this and he had nothing to add to what Jane already knew.

"Don't they go over the sites with a fine-toothed comb for clues?" Jane asked.

"Sure, and they found tons of unrelated junk. Sometimes that's all they find, but every bit of it has to be checked out. That's what's so damned time consuming. The dumpster is a real nightmare. Apparently it's a hangout back there. All kinds of beer cans, broken bottles, the butts of old joints, plus papers and stuff that may have been left by the murderer but probably just overflowed from the trash in the dumpster. They've got to check fingerprints on the damned thing with everybody who's remotely associated with the victims, the mall, and the trash-hauling company."

"That could take years! What about alibis?"

"John Wagner claims to have been home in bed both nights. His wife confirms it, but she would, wouldn't she? Chet Wagner—well, you know the situation with him the night his wife was killed, and last night he says he was tucked in at a hotel along with the other son. The other son, Everett, I think, confirms it. Everett, incidentally, seems to be in the clear for his stepmother's death. He was seen and photographed at some country house shooting party in Yorkshire. Of course, the sons could be lying, either to protect themselves or their father."

"What about Mr. Finch?"

"Same thing as the others. Says he was home in bed. Might be true, might not. None of the neighbors claim to have seen him leaving during the night, but apparently there were plenty of them who would have liked to pin it on him. Then there's the parents of the boy, the adopted parents, that is. Supposedly in Florida, and a humdinger of an alibi for last night. The father is a diabetic and got into some trouble with his blood sugar or whatever. Spent the night under observation at a hospital. Wife with him the whole time.''

They pulled into the school parking lot and, seeing that he was probably going to have to park in the next county, Uncle Jim let Jane off at the door and drove away in search of a spot. Jane walked slowly along the hallway, feeling very nostalgic. The school district music curriculum started at the fourth-grade level with two big concerts a year with all the kids from nine-year-olds on up. Jane had been coming here twice a year since Mike was that age. Steve had always hated coming, but she'd loved it. In fact, it was the one motherly duty that she saw as uncompromised pleasure. Unlike Cub Scouts or field trips or cheerleading practice, it required nothing of her except to show up and enjoy herself. And unlike many of the awards assemblies she'd sat through, it was truly enjoyable. Even the little kids learning violins and sounding like they were stepping on ducks had a certain charm that made up for the musical slaughter.

She found Thelma and the kids, and between them they managed to hold onto an empty place and flag down Uncle Jim when he finally came in. Thelma studied the program and started to point something out to Jane, who hastily said, ''No, I'm not supposed to know what's on it. I promised Mike.''

Huddled like a row of roosting chickens on the bleachers, they watched as the kids started to file in and take their places. Front and center were the two grade school groups. All the little girls had on their Christmas party dresses, and the little boys looked pink and shiny, like they'd been plucked from their baths only moments before.

Flanking these groups were the two junior high orchestras. The little guys had bounced into the gym; the junior high slouched self-consciously. The girls were well dressed in a terribly trendy, too-old way, and the boys were pretentiously underdressed. They were, as always, a funny mix of "shrimps and giants" as Jane had mentally dubbed this age group years ago. Some were still babies, others (usually the girls) had already shot up to adult height.

Finally, after these groups had settled into place, the high school group filed in. They were the only ones in "uniforms." The boys all wore black trousers and light green blazers with the school emblem on the breast pocket. The girls wore white blouses with a dark green vest and floor length skirts. True, a few of these skirts showed sneakers at the bottom, but on the whole, they were a spiffy group that came in with brisk, breezy self-confidence. They took their places in the semicircle of chairs set up behind the grade schoolers—more or less benevolent big brothers and sisters of the kids in front.

Mike took his place at the back, and as he looked over the audience, Jane managed to catch his eyes. She waved, and he nodded slightly in acknowledgment.

After a few inevitable announcements—"A silver-blue Oldsmobile Cutlass by the front door has its lights on," "Last chance for ordering a Fruit-A-Month from the fund-raising committee," "Cookies and punch in the all-purpose room after the concert," the program commenced.

The youngest went first, and Jane let her mind drift. Virtually the only way to recognize what they were playing was by consulting the program, and Jane wasn't allowed to look at one. How many times over the years had she sat here waiting for Mike's turn, wondering how it must feel to be the parent of one of those beautiful young adults at the back—and now she was one. And she'd discovered that these kids were as neat as they looked. She knew the band kids were often considered the nerds—Mike and his friend had rented a copy of *Revenge of the Nerds* one night and laughed hysterically at the last scene when the main character asks everybody at the high school assembly to bravely step forward if they're a nerd and the entire band comes forward in a group.

Still, they were good kids. She'd come to believe that if somebody took a national survey of the incidence of teenage crime in general and compared it to the incidence of teenage crime among those who were in musical groups, there would be a clear difference. Maybe certain kids got into such things because they are basically law abiding, but she preferred to believe they became that way because of the nature of the group effort. Even more than in team sports, a favorable performance resulted only from each one doing his assigned part as well as possible without anyone trying to hog the spotlight. If only boys like the late and not-very-lamented Bobby Bryant could be in school bands, they might turn out very different.

The grade schoolers got their just applause, and the junior high groups began. The contrast was impressive. This truly sounded like music—not good music all the way through, but it had its moments. They did a credible "Jingle Bells," which brought smiles to everyone.

Finally it was the turn of the high schoolers. Jane didn't recognize the first two numbers. They were the sort of thing teachers like better than audiences—pieces that were technically challenging to the students and made the director look good in the eyes of his peers, but nothing to hum along with. The third number was a light classical piece that Jane recognized but couldn't have named. Chopin, she would have guessed. When they finished, there was a significant pause. What could the last piece be that Mike thought she'd like so well?

The violin section raised their bows, staring as if hypnotized at the director for a long moment and at his signal began the initial slow strains of the "1812 Overture." Her favorite piece of music in the world! Jane looked at Mike, who was gazing back at her from behind his tuba with a wide grin. Dear God, if she were not feeling sappy enough already, this would finish her off before it was over.

She listened, mesmerized by their expertise. A musical expert would undoubtedly have found plenty of flaws in the performance; Jane found none. It was magnificent. The cannons were done on the big drum by a boy who had practiced playing as Scottish marching drummers did, with a string from the drumstick around the wrist to allow for fancy, dramatic twirling between beats. By the time the bells started—a very small girl bent over the xylophone—Jane was openly weeping, and so were many other mothers in the audience. Even the parents who had no high schoolers were stunned by the performance.

When the last low note faded, there was a long, electric silence before the entire audience surged to its feet, applauding wildly. Mothers pulled Kleenexes out of purses and wiped their eyes; fathers clapped for all they were worth; little brothers hooted and cheered approval. A few parents spilled onto the floor and looked like they could hardly resist the impulse to run and hug their kids, who would shrivel and die of embarrassment if they did.

Jim Spelling put his arm around Jane and hugged her close. "God, I'm proud of him," he said, his gruff voice sounding a bit choked.

Jane wondered how a day that started out with a funeral could possibly have finished so wonderfully. How could ugly, mean things like murder happen in the very same world where high school orchestras played the "1812 Overture"?

— 22 —

Jane got out of bed humming.

It was only eight o'clock, but she felt refreshed and wide awake, still in the afterglow of the band concert. She fixed a cup of coffee, fed the pets, and padded in slippered feet to the living room to have a quiet half hour of working on the afghan before she got the kids up for Sunday school. She became so engrossed in working on the last few rows that she lost track of the time. She wove the last loose thread into her creation, then spread it on the floor to admire it. What a shame she hadn't finished it earlier so she could enjoy it longer before having to sell it. It brightened not only the room, but also her spirits. Willard looked at the afghan and barked. She took it as a compliment.

"Do we get the morning off?" Mike asked, staggering in and sprawling bonelessly on the sofa. Max minced along the sofa back trying to determine what part of Mike's prone body he'd settle on.

"What do you—oh, quarter of ten! I don't suppose you'd go to the ten-thirty service with me, would you?"

"Nope. Do we have any orange juice?"

"Mike, in all your life have you ever known me to run out of orange juice? Toilet paper, yes. Butter, shampoo, light bulbs, cat food, clean sheets, yes. But never orange juice."

Jane let the other kids sleep in, and she and Mike

enjoyed a quiet morning together. Passing sections of
the Sunday paper to each other and gorging themselves
on sweet rolls, they didn't really talk much or about
anything important, but Jane felt the time with him was
probably more beneficial to both of them than a hectic
race to church would have been.

Quality time vs. quantity. One of those trendy pop-
psych phrases that sometimes meant a great truth and
most often were used as a cop-out by parents who
couldn't bother to make time for the kids. Like nature
vs. nurture. That was the most recent one, Jane thought
as she stacked up the rumpled newspapers and the
glasses that the orange juice crud was drying on. It was
an interesting concept. For years, if not generations,
mothers had been made to feel every fault a child
showed was truly their parents' failing. Recently the
women's magazines had been running pieces on the
opposite theory—that *none* of a child's problems were
the parents' fault, that people are born being what they
are, and nothing in their domestic environment can
change that basic character.

The truth had to be somewhere in between, or different for different people. But there must be something
to the nurture theory. How else could you account for
somebody like Bobby Bryant being Phyllis's son? Nobody ever mistook Phyllis for an intellectual, but at the
same time, there wasn't a mean or selfish bone in her
body. Bobby's creepy character certainly couldn't be
attributed to her genes. But that wasn't entirely fair to
some unknown adoptive parents. They wanted him and,
while Joan Crawford's daughter might dispute the point,
most people didn't go out of their way to adopt children
in order to mistreat them.

Then, too, it took two people to make a baby. Maybe
it wasn't Phyllis's genes, but those of the boy she'd been
married to so briefly. Jane wished now that she'd asked

more about him. What sort of kid was he? Phyllis had called him "ambitious and smart" or some such thing. Of course, from her sweet, simple vantage point, practically anyone could qualify for those adjectives. But could he have been a boy of strong character to let himself get swept into playing house? Hadn't he even the wit to wonder if Phyllis might have been pregnant—or didn't he care?

"Aren't you going to the door, Mom?" Mike shouted down the stairs. She'd been so deep in thought that she hadn't noticed her son leave the room, nor had she registered Willard's frenzied barking.

She opened the door to a blast of cold air and a Suzie Williams she'd never seen before. "Good God, you look like you've been stepped on by the cavalry," she said graciously to her guest.

"Thanks," Suzie croaked. Her face was pale but with hectic red circles on her cheeks, like a little girl who's been playing with her mother's rouge. Her hair, straggling out from a knitted hat, was lank. Her eyes were bloodshot, and she was mopping pitifully at a Santa nose. "I feel like shit," she said unnecessarily. "Could I come in, or are you going to watch me like a biology experiment while I die on your front porch?"

"I guess you might as well be in my house, since you haven't the common sense to be home in bed at your own."

Suzie staggered through to a chair in the kitchen. Collapsing in it melodramatically, she said in a voice that hurt to listen to, "A branch fell on the phone lines. I couldn't call. Jane, I need help."

"You need a doctor."

"I've called him and picked up the medicine already." She reached into her coat pocket and pulled out an orange plastic bottle full of capsules as proof of this statement. "But I'm supposed to sing in the church choir concert tonight."

"You not only can't do that, I'm sure you wouldn't even be welcome to try. You're spreading germs like Typhoid Mary."

"The point is, the physical arrangement of the choir is as important as the voices. We're standing on risers in a sort of pyramid. All I need is somebody to stand in my place."

"Oh, no—not me, Suzie. I can't carry a tune, and the director despises me."

"You don't need to carry a tune. Just silently move your mouth and stand in my spot. Jane, I'd do it for you," she added pathetically.

This little favor turned out to be a bit more trouble and a great deal more interesting than Jane anticipated. The sample items from the bazaar had been set up in the morning and then put away again, so she was there early to put them back out, which was a good thing. The choir director, a music major turned insurance salesman named Ed Shurran was understandably upset when she informed him that she would be standing in Suzie's spot but not—she assured him—singing.

"But you're a good five inches shorter than Mrs. Williams!" he said in a tone that verged on hysteria. "It'll spoil the whole look. And what about your robe? You'll be tripping over it in the processional."

Most of the church offices were closed and locked, and a hurried search didn't turn up needle and thread but did reveal a stapler and cellophane tape. Jane managed a decent job of temporarily shortening a robe while Ed Shurran stood over her, wringing his hands. She then draped and started arranging the display table as the choir members started arriving. As she was stashing the last empty carton under the table, Albert Howard came over to her. "I hear you're standing in for Suzie Williams. Poor old Ed has his knickers in a twist about it."

Jane chuckled at the English phrase. "With great reluctance, which is growing greater every second."

"Nothing to it. You're behind me in the processional and beside me on the risers. Come on. I'll walk you through it."

"That's awfully nice of you."

"No, it's self-defense. If I hang around the robing room, he'll try to sell me insurance. He always does."

They practiced their measured walk down the aisle and onto the stage. Albert showed her a list of the songs, all of which were familiar to her. She wouldn't have too much trouble mouthing the words. ". . . And you just follow me out," he finished. "Want to run through it again?"

"No, I think I've got it. Albert, I'm so grateful. This isn't going to be half as complicated as I thought."

They retired to the robing room with the others. Ed Shurran was talking to someone about collision and liability, and Albert Howard winked at Jane. When it was time, they lined up, and Jane had a momentary urge to hang onto the back of Albert's robe so she wouldn't lose him. "I'll get Suzie for this," she muttered under her breath.

Despite stage fright, Jane made it down the aisle and onto the risers without disgracing herself or the choir. Once they were into the second piece, she had calmed down. By the fourth, she was actually enjoying herself. As little talent as she had, she loved music, and it was downright thrilling to be standing in the center of all those lovely, powerful voices. It was especially nice that she was next to Albert. He had an awfully good voice. She'd always enjoyed his singing.

What a silly thought that was, she realized. She'd

never heard him sing alone. Only as an anonymous part of the choir. And yet, there was something so familiar in the tone, it was as if she'd listened to him many times before. How perplexing. When would she have heard him? Perhaps he'd had solos in church—no, she couldn't recall one.

"For unto us a child is born. . . ." the choir sang.

Jane was growing more puzzled. It was almost like knowing something once well understood but not being able to quite reach out and mentally grasp it. She concentrated on listening. The slight throatiness on the low notes, the infinitesimal quaver in the higher range, the continuity of the notes, without any obvious breaking for breath.

The choir paused between songs. The director, his back to the pews, grinned hideously, reminding them to smile. Jane grinned back.

"It came upon a midnight clear. . . ."

She stared at the back wall of the church, the better to focus her sense on listening. Maybe he just sounded like someone else. It would drive her crazy for days if she didn't figure it out. Somebody famous, maybe. She started mentally perusing a list of her favorite vocal tapes she had all over the house and car.

". . . to touch their harps of gold. . . ."

Suddenly Jane knew. He sounded just like Richie Divine!

But how absurd! Why would—how *could* Fiona's second husband sound so much like her illustrious first husband? Had he worked for years at sounding that way or—!

Glancing at him out of the corner of her eye, Jane studied those nondescript features. The hair was the wrong color, but that didn't mean a thing. Hair could be dyed or bleached. The pot belly? Age. The receding chin? The mustache added to the impression, which might have had help from plastic surgery. The mustache itself completely concealed the upper lip.

Albert Howard didn't *sound* like Richie Divine.

He *was* Richie Divine.

— 23 —

It took all the self-control she had to keep from turning and saying, "I know who you are! I love your records." Had they not been on stage in front of a lot of people, she would have.

As the last piece dragged on, however, she started having second thoughts. It was impossible. Richie Divine had been dead for years and years. He died when Katie was a baby. Fifteen years ago this month. Everybody knew that. But did they? Everybody knew his plane had crashed. She remembered her conversation with Mel about it. He'd said the plane and passengers were blown to so many pieces that nothing was identifiable. Was it possible that Richie Divine hadn't been a passenger on that plane?

If the man standing beside her actually was Richie Divine, he obviously hadn't died over the ocean when the plane exploded.

But why? How?

She almost missed her cue to step down. Albert Howard jiggled her arm, and she came to with a start and followed him down the risers. Trailing him, she noticed he was getting a bald spot on the top of his head. How sad that this golden idol of youth should have become paunchy and middle-aged in the obscurity of his own shadow. That *was* what he'd done—lived all these years as the pitiful second husband of Richie's wife. How terrible that must have been for him, to go from being an international superstar to an unknown nerd.

She almost spoke to him in the robing room, but didn't know what to say. It crossed her mind, too, that she had no business questioning him or even revealing that she'd inadvertently caught on to a very private secret. As she hung up her robe and went to repack the sample sale items, she recalled something Fiona had said about someone trying to get Albert to contribute to a project. The gist of the story was how insulted Albert had been at the implication that it was really Richie Divine's money, not his. Jane now understood the painful irony of the incident. Poor Albert must have felt the insult doubly.

The minute she got home, she phoned Shelley. "I made coffee cake this afternoon," she said seductively. "If you'll come over and eat some with me, I'll tell you something that'll knock your socks off."

"I'm not dressed. . . . Both socks?"

"Both socks," Jane assured her.

A moment later Shelley came in the kitchen door with a long car coat on over her nightgown and robe. She was wearing a pair of Paul's big snow boots, and there were curlers in her hair. "This had better be good."

Jane peeked around the corner. Mike was watching MTV over the top of his chemistry book. Todd was building a Lego space station. She knew Katie was upstairs on the phone. She put the coffee cake and plates on the table, and when they were seated, she said, *"The National Enquirer* would set me up for life for this information, which neither of us are ever going to tell anyone. Agreed? I don't think anybody but one other person in the world knows."

"Has this bazaar baked your brain? What are you babbling about?"

Jane lowered her voice and leaned forward. "Richie Divine didn't die. He's Albert Howard."

"What!"

"Shhh. I mean it. I stood next to him in the choir tonight, and since I wasn't supposed to sing, I just listened. Suddenly it hit me that I'd heard him before. I swear it's true, Shelley."

"Jane, as your friend—"

"I know, you think I've gone bats. But I haven't. Listen, that plane crash he was in—the plane blew up in midair, and the bodies were never found. Mel told me. His sister had been to the last concert, and he remembered the details."

Shelley leaned back, nonplused. "But why pretend to be somebody like Albert Howard?"

"I've been thinking about that. There was a story that the mob was after him for testifying against them. Mel told me that, too. I'd either forgotten that or never known it."

"That's why they planted a bomb or whatever on the plane," Shelley said. "I read about it in a magazine."

"Well, if he'd missed the plane for some reason, it would have been logical to go along and play dead. It was the only way to be safe from them in the future. If they'd known he'd lived, they'd have just kept after him until they succeeded."

"Oh, Jane. I don't know—"

"Shelley, if you'd heard him singing, you'd believe it. His voice is deeper now that he's older, but I swear it's the same man."

"But they don't look a thing alike."

"No, but neither does Sharon Kellick look like herself."

"Who in the hell—? Oh, yes. That woman down the

block who had the face-lift, and somebody called the police on her for housebreaking in her own house."

"Remember that show we saw on PBS a year ago about the plastic surgeons who work on severely malformed children? They made perfectly grotesque faces look normal. Imagine how easily someone like that could make a handsome face look ordinary. Richie Divine could have paid for the best doctor and bound him to secrecy. Maybe there was even a federal witness program then."

"I don't know, but they're not authorized to blow up planes."

"I didn't mean they did, but after it happened, he could have asked for help getting a good plastic surgeon."

"Okay, I'll give you that. But what about his hair? It doesn't look dyed, and I've never heard of a way to make your hair grow a different color."

"But it sure looked bleached when he was a star. Nobody who isn't an albino has hair that's naturally that blond. Maybe this is the color it was all along."

Shelley nibbled some cake thoughtfully. "Say, this is good. What about build? Albert Howard is sort of dumpy."

"Come on, Albert Howard is fifteen years older than Richie Divine was. Anybody can put on weight, even if age doesn't do it for them. Especially if there's an incentive like saving your own life. I could look like a blimp in a month without nearly as good a reason."

In spite of herself, Shelley was coming around to believing it. "Think about poor Fiona. All the horrible things the press said about her for marrying again so soon after Richie's death. And she took it all in silence. Now we know why. She wasn't marrying somebody else. She was remarrying Richie. She knows that, doesn't she?"

"She must. They married only a year or so after Richie 'died.' ''

They sat in silence for a long moment. Finally, Shelley said, "That's why Albert doesn't seem to mind that room you told me about. The shrine to Richie. It's a shrine to him.''

"Of course! I'd forgotten about that.''

"Do you suppose anyone else knows?''

"I'm sure they don't. Unless maybe a plastic surgeon. It's too big a secret to have been kept for so long by anybody but the two people most concerned with his safety. Albert and Fiona wouldn't dare let anyone know for fear they'd tell. It's like I said about *The National Enquirer.* You and I won't say anything about it, but lots of people would.''

"Oh, Jane. I'm almost sorry I know. It's going to kill me to keep this to myself. Just imagine, we *know* Richie Divine. It's like finding out your kid's guitar teacher is Elvis, risen from the dead.''

"Good comparison. I guess Richie could leave all the fame behind but couldn't stay away from the music. That's why he's in the choir.''

"That was taking a risk of discovery, wasn't it?''

"Not much. I don't think he ever does solos. And even though I'm absolutely bereft of musical talent, I've got an unusually good ear for it. I don't think many people could have made the connection. It's not as if the choir is ever going to do 'Red Christmas' and feature him. A different kind of music entirely must have seemed safe. And it has been.''

"It's a shame we can't ask Fiona about it. Find out how they carried it off. Why Richie wasn't on that plane. How it feels to have a weird secret like this.''

"I know. I'd love to talk to her about it. But we don't dare. It would scare her to death that we'd shoot off our mouths to other people. She doesn't know us well enough to trust us.''

"I don't know how I'll look at him again without gawking or accidentally calling him Richie.''

"You'll manage, Shelley, and so will I. We have to. In a way, we have his life in our hands. And we have to start tomorrow.''

"The bazaar! I'd actually forgotten about it for a few blissful minutes. Have you finished the afghan?''

"Yes, come look.''

When they went into the living room, Mike turned off the television and got off the sofa so Jane could spread out her work of art. After Shelley gushed for a moment, he said, "Mrs. Nowack, could I talk to you a minute? In the kitchen?''

Jane made a point of getting busy helping Todd pick up all the pieces of his project. Mike was undoubtedly asking Shelley about sizes for her. In the past, the kids had always consulted with Steve about shopping for her. Amazing how long a time it took to sort everything into new niches when one member of the family was gone. "Here I come!'' she said as she headed back to the kitchen.

Mike, grinning, told them both good night and disappeared. "Shelley, do you want to take some of this cake home? I made a double recipe.''

"I'd better. I need some reason to explain to Paul why I went tearing off in my nightgown. Other than the real one.''

"Now, remember, we can't tell anybody in the world about Richie Divine.''

"I promise,'' Shelley said.

Jane wondered if she could keep the promise herself.

——24——

On Monday morning, the bazaar began well. It had been a risk, having it so late in the year. Most craft sales took place in September or October, when people started thinking about Christmas shopping. The church committee had decided to catch people at the end of their shopping, when they had only a few gifts left to buy and were desperate to complete their lists. When Jane pulled into Fiona's driveway at eight-thirty, there were already a few cars parked on the street with women waiting for the bazaar to open at nine-thirty. It looked like the marketing ploy might just work. Fortunately, it promised to be an extraordinarily balmy day. That would help a lot.

Jane and Shelley doled out the signs to the group who had volunteered to post them. They went around to the various rooms making sure all the items were properly marked. Jane was to take the first shift in what they'd dubbed the "Wreath Room" because that's where most of those items had ended up. It was astonishing the things people made wreaths of; grapevines were the most popular, next to real or plastic pine boughs. But there were also wreaths made from pinecones, dozens of tiny foil-wrapped packages, and even one kitchen monstrosity made of pastel sponges tied in bow shapes and interspersed with dried flowers and miniature kitchen utensils.

Jane wouldn't have to actually sell anything. All sales took place at the long table by the front door where three women already waited. Everyone else did nothing more than stand around looking friendly and watching for shoplifters.

"It's amazing the things people will try to walk off with," Shelley said. "Last year I caught a woman stuffing a jar of potpourri into her coat pocket. It bulged like a horrible growth. I can't imagine she thought I wouldn't notice."

"It's astonishing to think people would take Christmas things from a church," Jane said. "What do you say to somebody who's stealing?"

"I just said, 'Let me take that to the front desk for you, and you can pay for it when you leave.' It worked; she hauled it out, slammed it down on the table, and stomped out as if I'd insulted her. I don't know what I'd have done if she'd denied it. What you have to look out for are the ones who come in pairs. One of them will engage you in a deep discussion about some item and stand so that you can't see what the other one is doing. That's why you need to be on your feet most of the time. So you can dodge around and keep an eye on everybody."

"I feel like a prison guard."

"Don't worry. There aren't that many who come to lift stuff. Mostly it's fun to stand around and gab with people. I guess it's time to open up."

There was a substantial line formed when they let people in. Some of the first were the barracudas—those canny shoppers, antique dealers among them, who came early and flew through fast with an eye out for an accidental bargain, something they could snatch up and resell at an inflated price. The quilt that had been marked so low would have been such an item if Shelley hadn't marked it up and purchased it herself. The early shoppers also included those women who were on their way to work and had to shop fast. The first hour, therefore, was hectic, but as the morning wore on, the pace became more leisurely, and Jane found herself enjoying the opportunity to visit with various neighbors she hadn't seen for a while.

At eleven, her replacement came, and she wandered off to the living room to see how Shelley was getting along. "My afghan's gone," Jane said, disappointed. It had looked so pretty draped over the piano, and she'd anticipated at least one last look at it.

"Yes, a woman bought it the first hour. Are you on a break? Suzie Williams was supposed to take over for me, and she actually had the grace to send a replacement. She's putting her coat away. I'll meet you in the kitchen when she's ready to take over."

The kitchen and family room had been set aside for the use of the workers. Signs on the doors said: STAFF ONLY. DO NOT ENTER. Jane went to the kitchen, got a cup of coffee and a croissant and joined Fiona in the family room. It was only the second time she'd seen her this morning, the first being when she let them in the house hours ago.

"It's going wonderfully well, isn't it?" Fiona said. "I was just speaking to the women at the front, and they say they've got nearly a thousand dollars already. Well, I better get along. I've got to stand guard on the ground floor guest bedroom."

"Oh, no, Fiona. I didn't assign you to that. We don't want you to have to do any more than you already have."

"It's quite all right. Ethel Besley called and said her car wouldn't start. I'm just taking her place until she gets here."

Jane made one more feeble protest, offering to take Ethel's duty, but was relieved when Fiona insisted on filling in. Jane desperately needed to sit down. She slouched into a comfortable leather sofa and nibbled her croissant as she stared at the pictures on the opposite wall. How different this room seemed now. The first time she'd seen it, she'd been shocked at the callousness of having a room devoted to Richie Divine that poor Albert had to look at every day and be reminded of his own lack of renown. Not it seemed a cozy, friendly place, a room where Albert and Fiona could recall the past while enjoying the safe, obscure lives they'd made for themselves.

"Jesus! This kind of thing brings out the best and the worst in people," Shelley said, coming in and flinging herself into a deeply upholstered chair. "I had a woman ask me to mark *up* a price, because it was such a good cause. Then I had a ghoulish threesome who made no bones about the fact that they'd come to see what they could ferret out about the murder next door. Didn't even pretend to want to buy anything, just asked me nasty questions."

"Probably undercover agents for VanDyne," Jane said. "I wonder if he's making any progress. It's terrible to admit, but I'd almost forgotten about it in the rush to get this thing going."

"Some detective. The day before yesterday you were going on about how you had the solution on the tip of your tongue. Now you've solved another little mystery, and you've forgotten the murders altogether."

"No, not altogether. I still think there's one little something that we already know that could unravel the whole thing. I just can't quite grasp it. As for the other—" She glanced over her shoulder to see if anyone else was around. "—that wasn't the solution to anything. It was just a stunning revelation of an interesting fact."

"Interesting? That's an understatement. By the way, where's Albert? I haven't seen him all day."

"Probably hiding from the ravening hordes. I can't blame him."

The question of Albert's whereabouts was answered for them a few minutes later when he came staggering in the back door with two Kentucky Fried Chicken barrels. "I thought the workers might need lunch," he said.

They stuffed themselves and returned to work. Jane took a two-hour shift at the front table, a busy job but one she got to do sitting down. When she was done with that and another hour filling in for a woman whose child had been sent home from school with chicken pox, she came back for another break.

There wasn't anyone in the kitchen or family room this time, and she was glad to be spared having to make conversation. Her voice was already getting fuzzy from all the talking she'd done. Her brain was getting even fuzzier. She sank back into the sofa, gazing sightlessly at the wall of pictures.

This had been one of the most frantic weeks of her life. Except for the quiet morning with Mike yesterday, she'd been running the whole time, ever since the day Phyllis and Bobby arrived. It wasn't just physical, it was mental exhaustion as well. Images of the past week were getting jumbled in her mind. Phyllis's body being taken away, setting up the bazaar, John and Chet Wagner yelling at Bobby, Mike's band concert, the church choir concert, the fight between Bobby and Mr. Finch, the funeral with Mel VanDyne rushing her past the news cameras. And someplace in all that mental rubble, there was something important they'd all overlooked. Something so small and ordinary that no one had noticed it in the pressure of the week's extraordinary events.

She was tired, almost nodding off, when her eyes suddenly focused on one of the pictures on the opposite wall. Without knowing quite why, she got up and went to look at it more closely.

Of course!

With a click she feared must be almost audible, things started falling into place. She stood back for a moment, stunned by what she was thinking. It could be. No, it *had* to be. Looking around to make sure she wasn't observed, Jane took the picture off the wall and stuffed it up under her sweater. Squeezing between shoppers, she went to the front closet and got out her coat and purse. Shelley was at the sales table. "Where are you going, Jane?" she asked.

"I've got to run an errand, Shelley. I'll only be a little while. It's important." Before Shelley could question her further, Jane ran out the door and headed for home. Once inside her own house, she took the picture out and studied it again. Then she dialed the phone. On the third ring, Mel VanDyne answered. "I've got it," she said. "At least, I've got half of it, and you can figure out the other half."

"Jane, what in the world—?"

"I have to meet you. How about that coffee shop in the mall? Here's what you have to do: Get hold of John Wagner, and have him meet us. Make him bring along that briefcase thing of Phyllis's with everything in it. I have to show you something in it."

"Jane, just tell me—"

"I can't. It's something you have to see, and I have to see it, too, to be sure I'm right. I'm leaving right now. See you there."

She hung up, stuffed the picture into a shopping bag, and headed for the mall. Before going to the coffee shop, she gave a bookstore clerk a tough five minutes finding a book she needed. Then, armed with her evidence, she dashed to the coffee shop and sat down to read hurriedly through the book while she waited.

25

Mel VanDyne and John Wagner arrived within moments of each other. Jane had taken over a corner booth which afforded relative privacy. "Please sit down," she said firmly.

The men exchanged looks that might have been surprise or amusement, but they did as she asked and sat down facing her. Jane noticed that VanDyne saw to it that Wagner was on the inside. Was that because he thought the man might try to make a getaway?

"First, I have to clear up a couple of things," Jane said to John Wagner. "How did you have a key to the house where Phyllis was staying?"

"She gave it to me," he said. Jane glanced at VanDyne, who stared back blankly. Apparently this was something that had already been cleared up to his satisfaction.

"Second, and I know this has nothing to do with the murders, but I want to know—have you ever met Albert Howard?"

"Yes, some time ago. I was trying to get him to contribute to building that park at the old Orville Wagner homestead."

"Orville Wagner? Any relation?"

"No."

That put to rest the discrepancy between how callous and tacky John Wagner had seemed to Fiona and how

agreeable he'd been during the course of the investiga-
tion. He hadn't been trying to name the project after
himself, as Fiona thought. Relieved, Jane took the picture she'd stolen out of her shopping bag and handed it
to John Wagner. "Now, this *is* to the point. Do you
recognize this?"

It was the band picture.

"Sure," he said. "Phyllis showed it to me dozens
of times."

"Yes, me, too, when we lived downtown so long
ago, but I'd forgotten until today."

"I didn't know she had a framed copy," John said.
"Why is this kid circled in the back row?"

"What is it?" Mel asked.

John handed him the picture. "It's a shot of the high
school band. Phyllis was one of the cheerleaders in the
front row. See, the second from the right. She was incredibly proud of being a cheerleader. It was one of the
high points of her life."

"So?" VanDyne said impatiently.

Jane said, "John, would you open her yearbook to
that page? Just to make sure. These band pictures look
so much alike. When I first saw it, I had the feeling I'd
seen it before, but I thought it was because they all look
the same."

John took the yearbook out of the needlepointed case.
It fell open to the page. The three of them studied it
carefully. It was identical.

"So what?" Mel repeated. "She had a framed shot
besides the one in the book."

"No, she didn't," Jane said. "The framed one is
from the Howards' house. Look at the yearbook. What's
the name of the boy in the top row who's circled on the
framed one?"

Mel took the book and ran his finger along the list

of names below the picture. "Richard Devane," he said.

Jane dragged out the book she'd just bought: *Richie Divine: A Star Extinguished.* She flipped it open to a page near the front she'd marked. She read aloud, " 'Richie Divine, born Richard Lewis Devane, was the second of two children of a middle-class Philadelphia family. He took an early interest in music. Drum and trumpet lessons from a neighbor paid off first when he got a position in his high school marching band.' "

"So you're saying this kid became Richie Divine, and Phyllis had gone to school with him," John said, perplexed.

"Not only went to school," Jane said. "I think she married him."

Mel had fumbled in his pocket for a small notebook. He flipped a few pages and looked up at her with amazement. "I had Bobby's birth certificate run down. She listed the father as Richard Louis Devane. Different spelling of the middle name, but maybe she didn't know there were two ways to spell it. Did she tell you she was married to him?"

"No. She only said they hadn't known each other all that well, and after the marriage was annulled, she'd never seen him again. No—no, that's not exactly what she said—" Jane closed her eyes, remembering the conversation. Phyllis had paused for a long time and said they'd never *met* again. Jane had thought at the time that she'd hesitated because she'd never considered the question Jane had asked. It wasn't that. It was a woman unused to lying trying to come up with a truthful, but misleading answer. And she'd succeeded brilliantly. They hadn't *met* again, but she had certainly seen him. Most of the world had seen him—on television, in a movie, posters, and record jackets. "She told me they had never met again. But that was before I took her over to Fiona Howard's house."

"God! She moved herself and Bobby into a house next door to the widow of his biological father," John Wagner said.

"Are you suggesting that Mrs. Wagner was trying to get something out of Mrs. Howard because she had given birth to Richie's son?" Mel asked. "From everything I've heard about her, it seems unlikely."

"No, that wouldn't have been possible for Phyllis," Jane said. "There's something else you have to know. I feel awful telling you, and you've both got to swear on your lives that if I'm wrong, you'll never, ever breathe a word of this to anyone. Promise?"

Both men nodded. It was obvious that they were surprised by the revelations so far, but not convinced they meant anything.

Jane leaned forward and spoke so softly they could barely hear her. "Phyllis didn't move in next door to Richie Divine's widow and her second husband. She moved in next door to Richie Divine and his wife. Albert Howard *is* Richie Divine. He didn't die in the plane crash. He was reborn as someone else."

"That's impossible," Mel said with a laugh.

"It isn't. Stop being so patronizing. You're the one who told me there weren't identifiable bodies found. The parts of the plane were never even accounted for. Remember?" Jane said.

"You mean he wasn't on the plane?" John asked. "Why not?"

"I have no idea. Maybe he just decided at the last minute to stay back with Fiona. It was almost Christmas. The next concert wasn't scheduled for three days," Jane said, tapping the book she'd bought. "It's all in here. Maybe they decided to let everybody think he was already in San Francisco and drive down the coast in a rented car without anybody knowing who he was. It could have been something like that. Then, when the accident happened, they saw it as an opportunity to be safe forever by keeping up the illusion that he'd been killed. There wasn't any problem with money. Royalties—or residuals, or whatever they're called—from his records would keep coming in for years, and Fiona would inherit everything he'd already accumulated—'' She stopped, sensing that she'd lost half her audience.

Mel was staring across the room. ''Or—or he could have known the bomb was on the plane.''

''What do you mean?'' Jane asked. ''He wouldn't have let the others take the risk if he'd known. And how could he have known?''

Mel gave her a long, level look.

John Wagner answered. ''He could have known if he'd arranged it.''

Jane nodded. It was a thought that had been swimming malevolently in the deepest, darkest part of her mind, but she hadn't allowed herself to recognize it.

The waitress, a perky girl with a gleam in her eye, bounced over to give them their bill. She tried to flirt with VanDyne but was firmly rebuffed. When she'd gone, John Wagner spoke again. ''So after years of hiding the truth and probably feeling pretty confident that nobody would ever discover it, he suddenly has Phyllis, his first wife, turning up.''

''Talking a mile a minute about her son, a boy exactly old enough to be Richie Divine's son,'' Jane said.

''How do you know she was talking about Bobby?'' VanDyne asked.

''I heard her. Sweet, gabby, completely indiscreet Phyllis,'' Jane said softly.

''And she recognized him?'' Mel asked.

''I think she must have, but maybe not right away. I'm sure he recognized her. When he came in the room, he looked like he'd been hit in the head with a hammer. I thought at the time it was because the room was such a mess, but it must have been the sight of Phyllis. Fiona had to force him to take Phyllis over to look at the house next door. He didn't want to. He was almost rude about it. But when he came back, he was really mellow. Like he'd sorted it out. Maybe they'd talked about it, and she'd agreed not to tell anyone.''

"She would agree," John said. "But I don't think she could have stuck to it. She was too open.''

"That must have occurred to him later," Jane said.

Mel said, "We've skipped over a vital part of this whole thing. Why do you think Albert Howard is Richie Divine? There's no resemblance. How would Phyllis have recognized him if the rest of the world hasn't? And what made you think of it?''

Jane told them about the church choir and elaborated on her theories about plastic surgery and age.

"But if you're right, it's only because you heard him sing and have a good ear. It doesn't account for Phyllis knowing him. I doubt that he hummed a few bars of 'Red Christmas' as he was walking her over to the house next door."

"But she knew him fairly well. She'd been married to him, if only for a short time. Besides, I think it's more likely that Albert himself gave it away. He knew her. He probably had fond memories of her, and he must have at least suspected that the son she talked about might be his. He and Fiona have no children. Getting to know a son is a powerful incentive for a middle-aged man to give himself away."

"And then have second thoughts about his own welfare," Mel said. He picked up the bill, glanced at it, and dug in his back pocket for his billfold. "All right, Jane. I think you've got something."

"That's big of you to admit," Jane said.

"Let me have all this stuff," he said to them. Jane handed over the framed band picture and the book she'd bought. John Wagner gave him Phyllis's yearbook. "I'm going back to the office to see what else I can run down. Mr. Wagner, I've got to ask you to keep this to yourself for a while longer. I know you're anxious to tell your father, but—"

"I understand. It might be raising false hopes. Besides, my dad might tear over there and try to take Albert Howard apart with his bare hands. Don't worry. I won't say anything yet. But when?"

"If there's any of this I can confirm, it shouldn't take more than a few hours," Mel answered.

"Just one thing," Jane said, scooting out of the booth. "Please don't ruin the bazaar."

"What?"

"It's only got a few more hours to run. We close down at six-thirty. A lot of people worked awfully hard on it. Please don't ruin it."

"Jane, you've got the weirdest priorities," Mel said. "All right. I won't make a move until six-thirty, but how am I going to explain that to my superiors? I'm sorry, boss, but I couldn't make an arrest until the last of the Christmas ornaments had been sold—"

Jane gave him a smile. "It's important to me."

"All right, but make sure you close down at exactly six-thirty."

John Wagner left them, and Mel walked Jane to her car. She paused with her hand on the door. "Mel, I don't much like myself for all this. What I've done to Fiona—"

He put his arm around her in a bracing manner. "It isn't what you've done, Jane. And you've got to think about your friend Phyllis, not Fiona Howard. You've done the right thing."

She looked up at him. "I know. It just doesn't feel very good."

Jane realized on the way back from the mall that she couldn't explain to Shelley what was going on. There wasn't the time or privacy to tell her the whole story, and it wasn't something to tell only a part of. The rest of the afternoon was endless. She stayed at the busy sale table in the front hall most of the time to keep her mind from endlessly circling what she'd done. She didn't see either Fiona or Albert all afternoon, but every time she heard a voice raised, she imagined it was Fiona discovering that the band picture was missing.

At quarter of five, she ran home for a minute. "Mike, drive me back to the bazaar, and you can have the car to get dinner. Here's some money."

"Aren't you going to be home?" he asked, grabbing his coat before she could change her mind.

"Yes, but not until later. I'll find a ride."

When she returned, some of the other workers were beginning to consolidate what was left of the sale items into two rooms. They also marked things down brutally. "Another rush will start any minute," Shelley said. "People on their way home from work. We have to unload everything we can."

At six, the last crew of volunteers set out to retrieve all the signs in the neighborhood. At quarter after, they put a CLOSED—SEE YOU NEXT YEAR sign on the front door and locked it. The few shoppers remaining picked over the last goods as the workers slashed prices right and left. At twenty after, Albert came through the hall in his coat and boots.

"Where are you going?" Jane asked. Dear God! Was

he escaping the net? No, of course not. How could he know?

"I put your cartons in the garage, and the roof has leaked. They're all wet, and you'll need dry ones to pack what's left," he explained. "I'm running up to the grocery store to get some."

"Oh, there's no need. I'll do it."

"No trouble," he said. "Is there something wrong? You look awfully pale."

"It's nothing. It's just been a long day."

She watched him leave, feeling helpless.

By twenty-five after, the shoppers were gone. Only Shelley and two other volunteers remained. "You can go on along," Jane told the other two. "Shelley and I can manage."

"But Jane—" Shelley began, but seeing the stricken look on her friend's face, she stopped. "Yes, Jane's right. We'll take care of packing up."

Jane saw them to the door and as she opened it, found herself facing Mel VanDyne. "It's six-thirty, isn't it?" she said needlessly.

He looked grim. "Mrs. Jeffry, would you ask Mr. Howard if I could speak to him?"

It was as if they were strangers. "He's not here. He's gone to the grocery store to get some cartons," she said in the same impersonal tone.

"Then perhaps I could speak to Mrs. Howard while he's gone."

Shelley came into the hall, smiling. The smile faded as she saw Jane and Mel facing each other with set expressions. "What's wrong?"

Mel turned to her. "Are you the only worker left besides Mrs. Jeffry?" Shelley nodded. "Would you mind leaving—quickly?"

"Of course. Jane, are you coming with me?"

"Yes."

"No," Mel said. "Not quite yet. I'll see that she gets home."

At that moment, Fiona came down the stairs. "Is everybody gone? How did we do? Would you like to help counting money or packing things—oh, it's Detective—uh—"

"VanDyne, ma'am. Could I have a few words with you?"

Fiona turned very pale. "Actually, it's not a good time. Perhaps later?"

"I'm afraid it has to be now," VanDyne said.

"Yes, very well," Fiona said, turning toward the family room.

Shelley watched her go, then mouthed to Jane, "Albert?"

Jane nodded miserably. Mel took her elbow and guided her along behind Fiona. Jane heard the front door close as Shelley left and had a mad urge to turn and run. Mel must have sensed the impulse. He tightened his grip on her arm. "I need a witness. My uniformed man slipped on the drive and is in the car whimpering over his wrist," he whispered.

When they entered the family room, Fiona was sitting on the sofa where Jane had sat earlier. She, too, was staring at all of the pictures. "Jane, there's a picture missing," she said in a small voice.

"I know. I took it," Jane said.

Fiona looked at her for a long moment, then said, "You know, don't you."

"Yes, Fiona. I know who Albert really is." Jane felt sick.

"What do you want?" Fiona said to VanDyne.

"I want to talk to your husband about the deaths of Phyllis Wagner and Bobby Bryant."

Fiona stood and walked to the wall, putting her palm on the spot where the band picture had been. Jane wished she could curl up and disappear.

"You don't, of course, have to talk to me at all," Mel was saying. "As his wife—"

She turned quickly and looked at him. "You don't need to talk to Richie. He didn't kill those people—I did."

26

"What!" Jane's exclamation came out as a strangled cry.

Mel practically shoved her into a chair and then turned back to Fiona, saying very smoothly, "Why don't you sit down, Mrs. Howard, and tell us about it."

Fiona shrugged. "I might as well."

"Don't you want to call a lawyer?" Jane asked.

Fiona ignored her. Mel had taken a card out of his jacket pocket and was reading her rights. She didn't act like she heard him or cared. He took a small tape recorder out of another pocket and put it on the coffee table. Pushing a button to start it, he said, "Do you understand that I'm recording what you're about to say, Mrs. Howard?"

"Yes, I understand."

"And you agree to be recorded?" Mel looked as surprised as Jane felt.

"Yes."

"Please tell me in your own words what happened," he said, slowly sitting down. He moved and spoke as if in the presence of a wild animal that might take fright and flee at any quick moves. Jane remembered him saying something days ago about needing a confession, because there might be such a lack of hard evidence.

Fiona glanced at him, then at Jane, then looked out

the windows and spoke in a flat tone. "Mrs. Wagner was my husband's first wife. The marriage was annulled, and he didn't know until last week that there had been a child. When she came here and I suggested that he show her the house next door, he recognized her. On the way over, she told him about her son—their son."

"Did Mrs. Wagner know right away who he was?" VanDyne asked.

"No. He told her. He *told* her," Fiona said. She looked years older, like the mother of a grown child who has done something very stupid. "You see, Richie isn't very good at—at protecting himself. He was so excited at the idea that he had a son, that he admitted to her who he was. It was very foolish. I couldn't trust anyone else to keep our secret. I've done so much all these years to keep everyone from knowing. Did she tell you, Jane?"

"No, she didn't tell me. I realized when I stood next to him in the choir."

"The choir. I told him not to be in it, not to take the chance, but he loved it so much. He really loved singing, you know. He didn't care nearly as much about the fame and the money as the sheer joy of singing. It was the only thing I couldn't give him. No, I didn't give him children, either. I think he would have liked children. . . ."

Her voice trailed off into a long silence. Mel broke it by saying softly, "So you killed her to keep the secret? Tell me about it."

"There's not much to tell. That night after Richie went to bed, I waited until the boy came home. I knew he was drunk from the way he was singing. I waited another hour to make sure he was sound asleep, then I went over there. I knew my way around the house from helping take care of the old lady who used to live there.

I almost went into the wrong room, but the boy was talking in his sleep, so I knew he had the big suite. I went in the small bedroom and killed her with a knife I'd picked up in the kitchen. I had one of my own with me, but I didn't want to use it.'' She leaned back in the chair and closed her eyes for a long moment. The only sound in the room was her breathing.

"Did you tell your husband what you'd done?" Mel asked.

"Tell Richie? No, of course not!"

"What about the boy? Bobby. Did you kill him, too?"

Fiona nodded. "I didn't want to. At first I didn't think it was necessary. Richie said the woman told him she'd never revealed to the boy who his father was. I thought that was probably true, but I couldn't be sure."

Jane shivered. Fiona was talking in a bleak but rational tone, as if they were discussing something serious but mundane, like the house needing a new roof.

"But then," Fiona went on, "then he started playing the music. It was all Richie's songs. Everybody thought he was just being a nuisance, but it was a message. I knew what it meant. He was saying that he knew who he was and who Albert was, and he was going to blackmail us. Richie had been so happy to find out that he had a son, but the son had no feelings for him at all. He—he was a blackmailer. He called after the police made him turn the music off and asked Albert if he'd heard it. I was on the extension, but they didn't know. He said he wanted to see Richie the next day and talk about an 'allowance.' That's what he called it. Richie was crushed. Absolutely crushed. So I called the boy back that night and told him Albert would meet him at the mall."

"Is that what you husband told you to do?"

"No, he didn't know I'd done it. Why do you keep

asking me if he knew? I didn't tell him anything. I took the same knife, and I got there early. He'd been drinking again, fortunately. I could smell it on him. If he hadn't, I don't think I could have surprised him so easily. I killed him."

Mel frowned. "If you'd like to get your coat, I'll have to take you in, Mrs. Howard. Once again, you understand that this tape will be entered in evidence at the trial—"

Fiona stood up. "There won't be a trial. I'm telling you I'm guilty. You don't have to prove anything. Nobody has to know why I did it."

"You can't continue to protect your husband's real identity," Mel said.

"Oh, yes I can. That's why I killed two people. I'd have killed twenty if it was necessary. Richie hated the slavering fans, the vultures, the mobs that wanted to pick him apart. Do you know—once, when he was Richie Divine, he went to a restroom in a hotel. Some horrible man rushed in and mopped up the urinal with a sponge and sold bits of the sponge." She shuddered with disgust. "I'd do anything to protect him from going back to being that kind of public figure. I've confessed. That's all you need, a confession. You have no reason to stage a circus for the press. I'd like to pack a few things. May I go upstairs and get them?"

"Yes. Do you want Mrs. Jeffry to help you?"

Fiona's spirit reasserted itself for a second. "No, I think Mrs. Jeffry has already done quite enough."

Mel cast Jane a quick sympathetic look and spoke again to Fiona. "By the way, I have men posted on all sides of the house. Don't think about escaping."

She smiled at him as if she pitied him. "It wasn't and isn't my intention, Detective VanDyne. I'm fully prepared to pay the price for what I've done. I knew I might have to before I did it. Just so Albert doesn't pay. It will only take me ten minutes or so to pack.''

As soon as she was gone, Jane jumped up and rushed to the sliding door. Stepping outside, she took several long, deep breaths, trying to stave off the nausea that had been about to overcome her. Mel was with her in a second. ''You'll freeze to death out here.''

''I hope so.''

He led her to a patio chair and made her sit down on the hard, cold metal. ''Put your head between your knees.''

''I'm not going to faint.''

''You're sure?'' he asked. She nodded and watched as he pulled a small walkie-talkie unit out of his pocket and mumbled into it.

The man's a walking electronics store, she thought wildly. She had an urge to laugh but knew it would get away from her if she let it start. She stood, shivering. Mel signaled across the yard, apparently to someone concealed in the bushes, then led her inside. He picked up a blanket folded across the back of a chair and wrapped it around her.

Just as he'd sat back down and looked at his watch, they heard the front door open. ''Where's everybody gone?'' Albert Howard called out. ''I've brought the boxes—oh, Jane, you're still here,'' he added, coming into the family room. ''What's the matter?''

Mel said, ''I think you should sit down, Mr. Howard. I'm afraid I have bad news for you. Your wife has confessed to the murders of Phyllis Wagner and Bobby Bryant.''

Albert just stood there at first, his mouth opening and closing like a fish out of water. ''What? That's crazy. Why would you say a thing like that? Fiona? My wife wouldn't kill anybody.''

''I'm afraid she has.''

"I don't believe a word of this. You've gone crazy. Where is she? We'll get this straightened out as soon as I call my lawyer."

"I think you should do that," Mel said. "Your wife is upstairs packing to go with me."

Albert sputtered for a moment more, then dropped his armload of paper cartons and ran up the stairs. They could hear his footsteps as he ran through the hall above, shouting for Fiona. He pounded on a door. Mel took the walkie-talkie out of his pocket again. There was a sudden sound of wood breaking. Mel barked a quick order into the gadget, then said to Jane, "Stay here."

But Jane followed him slowly. When she got to the bottom of the stairs, she heard a bloodcurdling man's scream. She knew she should do as Mel told her, but her legs seemed to be operating independently of her, slowly taking her up the stairs.

They were in the bathroom. "Stand back while I pull the plug," Mel was shouting.

"Fiona! Fiona!" Albert said, as Mel shoved him into the hall.

There was the sound of water splashing and a weight hitting the bathroom floor. Albert flung himself back into the room. "It's too late," Mel said.

Jane stopped at the doorway. Fiona, fully dressed and sopping wet, was lying on the floor. Albert was kneeling over her, trying to give her mouth-to-mouth resuscitation. Jane looked away. Mel came out just as three other men pelted up the stairs. "She filled up the tub and pulled a radio in with herself," he said. "Call an ambulance, and tell them to have something to calm the husband down."

Albert was sobbing. "Fiona! Fiona! Talk to me. You can't die. Fiona, you can't die. What will I do without you? Fiona! Answer me. Say something. Oh, God!"

One of the men went into the bathroom and started talking soothingly to him, another went back downstairs, and the third stood in the bathroom doorway, shaking his head. "I like to never," he said, bewildered. "She's in a bathroom, for Christ's sake. Why do it that way when she could have just slashed her wrists? Neater and faster."

"She wouldn't have done that," Jane explained, her voice shaking. "Fiona couldn't stand the sight of blood. She couldn't even hear about it without almost fainting."

Mel turned to stare at her. *"What did you say?"*

"Fiona couldn't stand the sight of—of *blood!"* Jane said. "Oh, my God, she couldn't have killed Phyllis!"

"Or Bobby," Mel added. "Oh, shit! Have I ever loused this up. She all but told us. She said she'd do anything to protect him."

Jane stepped over and looked in the bathroom door at Richie Divine clasping his wife's lifeless hand. "She gave everything she had for him. Even her life."

Mel edged past her and bent down. "Albert Howard, also known as Richie Divine, also known as Richard Lewis Devane, I arrest you for the murders of—"

Jane walked down the stairs and went into the family room. She stared for a long time at the dime store strip of photos of Richie and Fiona. If only she could fill her eyes and mind with those two happy, hopeful young faces and forget the dead woman and the murderer she had died to protect in the upstairs bathroom.

27

The next morning Shelley came over to hear what had happened while Jane put away groceries from a hasty pillage and plunder visit to the grocery store. Jane spoke disjointedly as she rearranged the contents of the refrigerator to make room for new items.

"You're driving me mad! Let the nonperishables wait," Shelley finally insisted. "Come sit down, and tell me everything." They took steaming cups of spiced tea and packaged cookies into the living room. "Jane, you've put your tree up! When did you have time?"

It was an enormous tree, and the cats were frolicking among the boughs, making the ornaments rattle. "The kids got it yesterday afternoon and even decorated it. Katie beat the boys into it, because it was always Steve's job. I shudder to think what she's got on them that she could make them go to all that trouble. I'm very suspicious of that big package."

"Which one?" Shelley asked with wide-eyed innocence.

"This one. It's huge and squashy. It feels like a blanket or an—an *afghan*! Shelley, you bought me my afghan!"

Shelley feigned outrage. "I certainly did not. Look at the tag."

"It's from the kids. Oh—that's what Mike took you

aside to talk about when you were over here Sunday night.''

''I'm not admitting anything.''

Willard, trying to adjust himself comfortably with his chin on Jane's lap where he might pick up any cookie crumbs that dropped, suddenly sat up and howled horribly. Jane went to the door and let Mel VanDyne in.

''Thought you'd want to know you can get back into the Howards' house this afternoon if you need to clear things out from your sale. Hello, Mrs. Nowack.''

''He's confessed, then?'' Jane asked, moving her coat and Shelley's off Steve's old favorite chair so Mel could sit down.

''Has he ever. Once he got started, he didn't seem to be able to stop. He'll probably go to a mental hospital instead of jail. At least the press hasn't found out about this yet. It's going to be a three-ring circus when they catch on that Richie Divine is alive and about to be locked up.''

''I feel awful about this,'' Jane said. ''If I hadn't dragged Phyllis over there in the first place—''

''You can't blame yourself, Jane. Killing people wasn't new to him. He's confessed to arranging for the bomb on the plane as well. He let a half dozen people die so that he could be Albert Howard.''

''Poor Fiona,'' Shelley said.

''Oh, I don't know. He's trying hard to absolve her, but the more he talks, the more it seems she was responsible. Not that she actually planned any of it, but it was she who convinced him he had to escape the public spotlight at all costs. I'm not sure he's the one who hated it. And without her, he has no sense of self-preservation at all. Of course, killing the boy was different—''

''His own son,'' Jane said with a shudder.

''Yes, but that was why. It wasn't just the blackmail

threat. It was the very fact that Bobby *was* his son. Instead of looking up to his famous father, he was ready to betray him. Threatened to go to the papers, tell everybody, blow the cover the Howards had so carefully built up. Richie—or Albert—couldn't stand that. All those years of self-imposed, or Fiona-imposed, obscurity, then the one person he wanted to impress turned it on him.''

"How extraordinary. Just think of all the people in the world who would give anything for fame, and yet Richie and Fiona had it and were willing to break all the rules of civilization to escape it. Andy Warhol should have added something to that fifteen minutes of fame business to the effect that fifteen minutes is all that's good for anybody. Oh—I have something for you,'' Jane said. She got up and dragged a plastic bag out of the cabinet below the bookshelves. "Phyllis left her knitting here. She was working on a sweater for Bobby.''

VanDyne looked at the lumpy bag. "So? She knit a clue into the pattern? Wasn't that *A Tale of Two Cities*?''

"In a sense she did.'' Jane rummaged in the bag and pulled out a hardback knitting book of stitch patterns. From between various pages, scraps of yarn and corners of loose papers hung out. "She left it here. I got it out last night to see if I could finish the sweater,'' Jane explained, flipping through the pages until she came to what she wanted. She took out several typed pages stapled into a blue folder and handed it to Mel.

"The will!'' he exclaimed, taking it from her. "Had she changed it in Bobby's favor?''

"I don't know. I didn't read it. I was already so far over my snooping quota that I didn't feel I had the right,'' Jane said. "How rude of me! Would you like some tea and cookies?''

"I thought you'd never ask."

"I've got to go," Shelley said, following Jane to the kitchen. "Are you going to invite him to Christmas dinner like you said?" she whispered.

"Quit nagging. All in good time."

"Before the new year?"

"Get out," Jane said, opening the door for her.

When Jane came back to the living room with Mel's tea, he was just glancing over the last page of the will. "Bobby would have been disappointed. She left him a lifetime trust with approximately a thousand a month income. Enough to help him through, but not enough to live on in style. It reverts to her husband."

"I'm so glad to hear that—that she had good sense in spite of seeming so stupid about him."

"You fared better than Bobby did."

"Me? What do you mean?"

"She left you twenty thousand, outright."

"Dollars? Twenty thousand dollars?" Jane said, putting the tea tray down with a clatter. "Imagine Phyllis doing a thing like that."

He took a sip of tea and leaned back. "Well, if that money were mine, I'd go looking for some sunshine over the holidays—Bermuda, maybe."

Jane took a deep breath, gulped, and said as casually as she could manage, "Then you don't have plans for Christmas? Would you like to have Christmas dinner with us?"

"What? And miss a microwaved frozen dinner by myself?" He grinned. Oh, that almost-dimple! "I'd love to join you. Say, I'll even bring along dessert. Somebody at the office gave me a fruitcake. . . . What are you laughing about?"

JILL CHURCHILL is a pseudonym of historical novelist Janice Young Brooks. A lifelong mystery buff, one of her most treasured possessions is a personal letter from John Dickson Carr. She has knitted a great many tubular objects because she can't purl and has to keep going in the same direction.

JILL CHURCHILL

"JANE JEFFREY IS IRRESISTIBLE!"
Alfred Hitchcock's Mystery Magazine

Delightful Mysteries Featuring Suburban Mom Jane Jeffry

GRIME AND PUNISHMENT
76400-8/$5.50 US/$7.50 CAN

A FAREWELL TO YARNS
76399-0/$5.50 US/$7.50 CAN

A QUICHE BEFORE DYING
76932-8/$5.50 US/$7.50 CAN

THE CLASS MENAGERIE
77380-5/$5.99 US/$7.99 CAN

A KNIFE TO REMEMBER
77381-3/$5.99 US/$7.99 CAN

FROM HERE TO PATERNITY
77715-0/$5.99 US/$7.99 CAN

SILENCE OF THE HAMS
77716-9/$5.99 US/$7.99 CAN